the Boy Scout handbook, and the value of hearing from a trusted adult after you have done something nominally bad, like punching a bully or defying an eldritch villain, 'You done good.'" —Adam-Troy Castro, author of the *Gustav Gloom* series and *Z is for Zombie*

ACRES OF PERHAPS

"Evocative tales of alternate realities steeped in the ethos of Shirley Jackson and Ray Bradbury." —Kirkus Reviews

"Imagine *The Twilight Zone* with a beating heart, Hitchcock crackling with strangeness around his edges. This is masterful storytelling for fans of literary and genre fiction alike." —Michael Wehunt, author of *Greener Pastures*

"Ludwigsen has a talent for constructing atmosphere without overwhelming the reader with concrete descriptions, and he is a deft observer of what shadows move the human heart." —Jack M. Haringa

IN SEARCH OF AND OTHERS

"Each story's concepts remain fully accessible while still challenging the reader, and exquisite craftsmanship makes this a timeless classic for those seeking asylum from formulaic prose." —Publishers Weekly, starred review

A SCOUT IS BRAVE

Also by Will Ludwisgen

Acres of Perhaps: Stories and Episodes

In Search of and Others

Cthulhu Fhtagn, Baby! and Other Cosmic Insolence

Will Ludwigsen

A SCOUT IS BRAVE

Published in 2024 by Lethe Press
www.lethepressbooks.com • lethepress@aol.com

Cover design and layout by JeremyJohnParker.com

ISBN: 978-1-59021-660-6

For William Simmons, *who was never to my knowledge a Boy Scout but who has exemplified every one of their stated ideals throughout our nearly forty-year friendship...though not perhaps in the ways they'd expect. I appreciate our late-night urban hikes and the honest perspectives you've always provided to me. I hereby award you the Iconoclastic Integrity merit badge.*

I

When 1963 started, it was still possible to be an idiot about the world if you were thirteen and didn't know much about it. The missiles in Cuba were gone, 122 Americans would be killed that year in Vietnam, and when you clenched your eyes tightly enough, you could pretend black people were getting bludgeoned only in Alabama.

My Scout handbook had a Norman Rockwell cover with a cheerful waving boy on the front, and he was holding another handbook with another cheerful waving boy on the front, and so on into infinity, which was just how much I believed every word in it: forever and ever, amen.

By the time we moved from Queens to Innsmouth that summer, though, I was beginning to think my father might be right and only suckers like me believed in being trustworthy and loyal and all the rest. Mom had lost a baby in March and Dad had lost his job in April, and there's not much more you need to know about how crummy our lives had gotten than it was an improvement to move to a crumbled pile of rocks on the bleak Massachusetts shore.

Well, almost nothing more to know.

It was in Innsmouth where I met the greatest Scout I've ever known, a boy named Aubrey Marsh, and he's the reason I'm still here and the reason I still believe it's worth being human, even though he's not quite either of those things anymore.

2

If you've never heard of Innsmouth, that's okay; it's a sure sign you're living an enviable life of happy ignorance. We wouldn't have heard of it either if Mr. Farkas from the Innsmouth Oil Speculating Consortium hadn't called my dad one morning in mid-June with a job offer we were desperate enough to take.

My father was a construction and demolition diver, a Sea Bee during the war, and he worked a lot of jobs building or clearing bridges and piers all over the New York and New Jersey coasts. He'd suit up in a heavy canvas outfit with a brass helmet to either weld steel or blow it loose with Primacord, which sounds like a cool job until you realize it meant spending hours a day in the East and Hudson Rivers breathing oil-rancid air down a hose.

My dad hadn't been working since April. On his last job, he was forced to take on a supervisor's son as an "apprentice" so he could be plausibly added to the payroll. One day the guy wandered off during my father's dive and the compressor stalled. When that happens, the rancid air stops and all you have is what's left in your helmet to get to the surface.

When Dad finally made it back up, he flung his helmet across the deck like a bowling ball and told the boss to fire his kid. Instead, it was my father he sent packing, which is how Dad was home reading *Atlas Shrugged* on the couch in his undershirt at nine in the morning to receive the call from Raymond Farkas, Esquire.

As Dad told it later, Mr. Farkas asked to speak to "the best underwater demolitions man on the eastern seaboard," which was a smooth way to start. I remember my father waving at Mom and me to be quiet even though we were both reading in silence on the couch. We looked up and listened to Dad's side of the conversation, which was mostly him saying, "Yes," and "That's what I do," and "When can I start helping you?"

The seaside town of Innsmouth had fallen on hard times, Mr. Farkas told my father. Once a center for shipbuilding and fishing dating back to the 1700s, the town suffered several catastrophes soon after the turn of the century that closed its fish packing plants and scattered its last few residents for good. But nothing dead stays dead forever, Farkas said, and hope was sprouting once again in Innsmouth. Or more accurately it was bubbling, as in the persistent seepage of crude oil detected offshore by a geology firm.

When my father got to this part of the story after the call, Mom was surprised. "Have you ever heard of oil in Massachusetts?" she asked.

"No," he said. "But then, the name of the company includes the word 'speculating,' right? What's wrong with helping them speculate?"

What Innsmouth wanted from my father was to move our

family to their town and help install the second-hand oil drilling rig they'd towed from the coast of Venezuela to about a mile offshore. For his crucial contribution of six months' construction and demolition work, the investors were willing to pay all our moving expenses (both ways, if we didn't choose to stay after the project was done), a house rent-free, and a salary of $30,000.

"That can't be right," Mom said.

"Look, it's probably to make jobs for the locals," Dad said. "If a bunch of fat cats want to throw their dough around to save the town, what's wrong with letting them save us, too?"

In our little Flushing apartment, we were broke and sweltering and losing our minds, which must be why my mother let her keener practical faculties give way. Thinking back on it now, though, she was the one who'd been the most restless of the three of us, going in and out of what would have been the nursery, sitting out on the fire escape with an ashtray full of butts, and winding down slowly like a clock. I didn't guess it then, but she needed a change more than any of us.

As for me, I had nothing keeping me in New York, either. Sure, I'd lived there all my life, but it wasn't like anybody wanted me to stick around anymore.

"What about Bud? He has school here and friends," Mom said.

Before I could tell her it was fine, Dad said, "You mean those comemierdas he had to tune up on?"

I'd seen Jaime and Frank a few times in Kissena Park after my disastrous last Scout meeting, but they'd walked away as though I should be embarrassed to show myself. I was, but they never gave me the opportunity to un-embarrass myself with an apology. So when school started again I'd have to find new friends, which I figured would be just as easy in Innsmouth as New York. Easier, maybe, with no past for the new kids to know about.

"You know, I think a change would be good for all of us," I said.

"See?" Dad said. "Chance of a lifetime. It's like the stars have aligned."

We moved two weeks later at the end of June, and though we didn't peel out from the curb in Dad's Volkswagen bus, we didn't take a nostalgic turn around the park or stop for an egg cream, either. While the movers went on ahead with their truck full of our things, Dad squeezed Mom's hand before pulling it uncomfortably over the shift lever, and they both smiled through the windshield as we pulled away.

Only I looked back, which is how I saw Jaime (arm still in a sling) and Frank (left eye still blackened) watching us leave from the sidewalk, satisfying themselves I was gone for good. They didn't wave, and neither did I.

3

You can drive from New York City to Innsmouth in one long day if you don't stop much to eat or pee, but that's just distance. In terms of time, the decades fall away as soon as the buildings of New York are behind you, first to the smaller cities and towns of Connecticut and then to the villages and lonely farms of rural Massachusetts. Some of the places we passed could have come from the Scout handbook with their bandstands and general stores, but what we noticed most was the quiet. It was a little like driving into a dream, and we didn't talk much on the way.

We reached the shore and headed north just as the afternoon was darkening toward evening, and after an hour of roughening road, we came to the top of a hill. Dad stopped the VW, and through the windshield we could see Innsmouth sprawled before us, larger than we'd expected but emptier, too. The outward edges of town seemed ragged and crumbling, full of old gray houses on old gray streets shaded by old gray trees.

"The whole town is a fixer upper," Mom said.

"It's a hellhole, is what it is," my father said.

We descended the hill into town along Federal Street past

rows of houses sagging from the weight of dampness, their wooden porches dark and rotting, their bricks covered with moss. You don't think of New England as a swampy place, but Innsmouth sits low along the shore in a marsh and the moisture seems to wallow there.

We soon came to a town square with a freshly-scoured First National grocery store and a fire station, and the people running their afternoon errands stopped to wave at us. They all seemed older than my parents, most with gray hair, and they wore the clothing you'd expect from a small town: the firemen played checkers in their red suspenders, the manager of the market stacked cans in an apron. A woman in sagging stockings trundled along the sidewalk with a bag of groceries, but there wasn't time to jump out and help her.

We crossed a walled-in river (the Manuxet, we'd later learn) on a crumbling bridge and passed through another square, and here Mom had to check our directions again to direct us to turn first at Church Street and then onto Adams. That's where our house was waiting for us, along with a dozen townspeople beneath a hand-painted banner reading "WELCOME CAS-TILLOS."

Dad had barely pulled the parking brake before people started opening the doors of the Volkswagen bus. Two older ladies in blue dresses helped my mother from the passenger seat, and a heavyset man in a sweaty white dress shirt and suspenders hurried to my father's side. The guy looked like he was just betting on the ponies at Aqueduct, complete with a little brimmed hat.

"Raymond Farkas," he said, holding out his hand. With each word, his tie twitched against his bulging neck. "I guess you'd call us the Welcome Wagon."

Dad shook his hand. "Ted Castillo," he said, distracted by the people crowding around to put much strength into it.

"We know," said Farkas.

Dad nodded up toward the house standing two stories above us with a long porch curled around the front and side. "It's a beautiful place," he said, meaning only the house, which had been restored at a higher priority than the rest of town.

"The Reverend insisted we find you a special one," Farkas said. "A lot of them around here are, after a little elbow grease."

If my father was curious about who Farkas meant by 'the Reverend,' it wasn't for long: a tall man in a salmon-colored suit, the brightest thing in Innsmouth, emerged onto the front porch and raised his arms like he was about to part the Red Sea.

"Folks!" the man shouted, motioning the crowd to quiet down. "Today we welcome a new family to ours!"

The people whooped and shouted in a muted New England sort of way. Like the ones in town, they wore older clothes, dark and formal, yellowed at the sleeves and rumpled. Many women had lacy necklines, and many men had drooping fedoras.

"I'm Reverend Pritchett," he said, "and as you can tell by my accent, I ain't from 'round here."

That got a laugh from the crowd. He sounded Southern to me, though his voice had a flat quality I couldn't place.

"Like you, though, I was lucky enough to find my way to Innsmouth." Some people started to cheer again, but Pritchett raised his hands. "And though we weren't born here, I figure you'll learn like I have that home ain't where you're from but who you're with."

The crowd shouted their agreement.

My parents kept smiling, but I could see Dad rattle the watch on his wrist, his usual sign that he was ready to move on to something more constructive. Nobody caught it but me, though, so he settled on his heels.

"Back home New Orleans way, my mama liked to put together them jigsaw puzzles, you know the ones, spreading 'em out on our old kitchen table and snappin' pieces in one by one, like the Spivey sisters do in that beautiful parlor of theirs."

Two older women in front, the ones who'd helped my mother, beamed in their recognition.

"Now Mama did this real special thing for me every time. She'd always save the last piece for me. Took a lot for her give away her satisfaction that way, but I loved the little shiver I'd feel when a piece fit in on all four sides. I'm feeling a little shiver today. Aren't y'all?"

A few people in the crowd shouted, "Amen!"

"Today, with the arrival of the Castillos, we're completing Innsmouth's bold new picture!"

Everyone applauded, even my parents.

When the noise faded, Pritchett motioned to his left. "Now, y'all got nothin' to worry about. Dinner has been taken care of by the Ladies Auxiliary."

Three old oak-skinned ladies stood holding covered plates with stoic pride, or maybe total indifference. It was hard to tell.

"As for your heavy lifting," Pritchett continued, "the rest of us will handle that."

The people cheered again and then turned toward the moving truck. It had arrived before we did, God knew how long, and the movers sat waiting in the cab with their cigarette smoke rolling out the windows. Now, their mouths fell open as the horde lurched towards them.

One of the Innsmouth men fumbled at the rear door latch, and a few more shoved the door open with a clang. Then, like ants swarming the corpse of our former life, the people of Innsmouth marched in and out of our house, carrying our dressers and tables and chairs. They knocked a few into the walls, of course, and they broke a mirror after a spectacular drop from the top landing on the stairs. They got Dad's chair lodged in the doorway for half an hour while three men with sweaty foreheads argued over how to get it out. Still, we were politely grateful for their "help."

The professional movers tried to steer clear of the swarm. They lifted our larger items out of their reach and scurried in and out of the back door. "Gangway!" they cried, holding our couch overhead like pygmies portaging a canoe. People scattered whenever they approached.

The truck emptied far faster than it had filled, and Mom was harried by their speed. She worked as a traffic cop, directing people all over the house on where and how to set things down. I don't know which phrase she said more often: "Over there, please," "Look out," or "That's okay, it wasn't valuable." She was relieved, though, when the last of our boxes entered the house and all of the townspeople exited.

Two of the movers slammed the back doors shut while the third handed a bill to my father. Dad barely had time to reach for his wallet, though, before Pritchett intervened.

"Now, now. The Innsmouth Oil Speculating Consortium's got it," he said, giving a nod to Farkas who handed the wide-eyed moving man a roll of fifties.

With everything now stacked inside and the truck rolling out of our driveway, all the "helpers" formed a line to shake our hands and welcome us to town, and I've never felt so many wobbling and papery hands. Then, tipping their hats, they went away in ones and pairs, walking down our street in a quiet procession.

"Aww," Mom said, watching them amble away. "How can we ever repay you?"

"Well, Ma'am," Pritchett said, "you can always honor us with your presence at the Evangelical Progress Temple."

"Oh, we'd love to," Mom said. Dad coughed.

"Well, you folks get yourself situated. If you need anything, pretty much anybody in town will help you, but I'm living in the parsonage behind the church on Federal Street." He pointed toward a spire visible in the distance above the trees. "Can't miss it!"

Pritchett turned and followed his people back toward the center of town as dusk began to fall. He put his hands in his pockets and started to whistle.

"That's the weirdest damned thing I've ever seen," muttered my father.

"Maybe people in Massachusetts are just friendly," said Mom.

Dad winced. "Jesus, I hope not."

4

The Innsmouth Oil Speculating Consortium didn't expect my father to start work the next day, but Dad wasn't going to be comfortable nesting at home with Mom and me when a new job was waiting for him a mile out in the harbor. By the time I made it down to the kitchen that first morning, he was already screwing on the cap of his Thermos and tucking it under his arm.

He let me carry his heavy brass helmet out to the Volkswagen. Inside already were neat coils of orange hose wrapped around his portable compressor, and I set the helmet on the floor by the front passenger seat. I wondered if he'd get to dive that day, and whether the sun would warm him under the water.

When he kissed my mom on the porch in her pajamas, she said, "Try not to get fired yet."

"Funny," he said, though smiling. Then he turned to me. "You gonna help your mom out today?"

"Sure," I said. "I don't think you should get fired either."

"The usual peanut gallery," he muttered, climbing into the bus.

After he left, Mom and I spent the morning unpacking and setting up the house. Our own furniture from the apartment filled three rooms, but there were old velvet-covered chairs and sofas left behind by the last owners to fill it out. They puffed out dust when you sat on them.

My bedroom was a finished attic with a cool sloping ceiling, heavy beams, and gable windows. It didn't take long to set up my desk and my books or to hang the B-25 bomber model from its fishing line. On the walls, I placed my shellacked sample knot board I'd made in summer camp and tacked up a few maps from *National Geographic*. In just a few years, I'd remember it with shame as the room of a total square, but maybe there was hope for me in some of the books, at least: *Catcher in the Rye, Live and Let Die, The Martian Chronicles, Lord of the Rings*.

Hidden between the mattress and box spring was a copy of *The Feminine Mystique* that I'd filched from Mom when she was done with it. I hadn't gotten to any juicy parts about how women worked yet, but I had learned it was really, really boring to be a housewife. Mom still wasn't quite back to herself yet, but she was downstairs setting up the easel and drafting table she'd used when illustrating advertisements for magazines, which seemed a good sign.

Around ten, I was straightening lamps and fluffing cushions so Mom would take the hint I was done. She finally did.

"Go on," she said, waving a hand listlessly in my direction. "Explore and conquer."

I took my bike out of the carriage house and started off toward downtown to see what was shaking, as we said back then. Mostly it was me because the streets were barely usable, most either missing bricks or cracked by the grasping roots of elm trees, and my Schwinn bucked me like a bronco at each pothole.

The few people I saw that early, sitting on porches or tending to their yards, all waved to me like old folks do, with a hopeful smile that you'll stop to listen to them. It was hard to wave back with both my hands clutching the handlebars, but I kept going. There'd be plenty of time to chat with them later.

In total on my ride, I counted six operating businesses. The Provident Bank wasn't open yet, of course. Outside People's Drugs, a pharmacist in a lab coat swept the uneven sidewalk. Through the windows of the First National grocery store, I could see a guy with a paper hat stocking cans on one of the four aisles of shelves. Signs on the front of the hardware store advertised a special on mason jars, and a greasy spoon diner next door called the Innsmouth Cafe smelled of bacon and sausage. At the entrance of the Innsmouth Oil Speculating Consortium offices, Mr. Farkas had tucked his briefcase between his knees so he could hold his coffee and his keys at the same time to unlock the door.

As for civic services, there were even fewer: a post office with a single window for customers, a jail with an old Nash cop car out front, and the fire station we'd passed on our way into town. A couple of pot-bellied volunteer firemen stood hosing down the ladder truck, and they gave me a manly nod as I passed.

Almost everything else was boarded up – the consolidated school, two other banks, a newspaper office, and at least four churches. It was like these people had discovered this town and didn't quite have all the furniture to fill it yet, just like my family couldn't fill our house.

The Evangelical Progress Temple was the only open church in town, a white stone building that looked like a bank with four columns out front. I couldn't tell if it was Baptist or Presbyterian or Lutheran or what. Reverend Pritchett was mowing the lawn in dress slacks and rolled up sleeves, and he gave me a thumbs up as I passed that I returned because a Scout is courteous, even when he's a little creeped out.

What troubled me was that there were no signs of other kids, no hopscotches chalked on the sidewalks or playgrounds with rusty merry-go-rounds creaking in the breeze or bikes left propped against trees. The simplest explanation was most of the folks in town were old enough to be grandparents, but it was still a disappointment.

As a last-ditch try, I found the library. Back in Flushing, I used to get ragged for being the kind of guy who liked reading about camping as much as doing it, but the truth was people did things right in books, not all half-assed and selfish.

The library looked like one of those Carnegie jobs, a marble cube with columns and steps leading, of course, to planks nailed across the doors.

Now, the Scout handbook doesn't forbid breaking and entering, and you could tell yourself that exploring a building wouldn't be much different than exploring the woods, as long as you left no trace. So I tucked my bike into the bushes and walked around the building to, you know, investigate my options.

Toward the rear corner, I heard a creaking noise. I froze and then crept forward, rolling each foot gently from heel to toe to walk in silence like the Algonquin tribe used to do. That's how I found the boy whose foot was sticking out from under a sheet of plywood covering a back window.

I watched as the foot and shoe – a dressy brown loafer, to my surprise – wiggled and turned and began to descend with the legs following after. The pace quickened, and a boy dropped out like a spoonful of cookie batter to land in the leaves.

He had three books in his hand held together by a belt, and he bent to sweep the dust from his pants. He must have caught sight of me from the corner of his eye because he recoiled and let out an odd gurgling shriek that I have been able to imitate now from then to now, something you'd spell with a lot of A's and maybe some G's and H's.

He stumbled back, slipped in the wet leaves, and landed on his can. He scrambled backward a moment but stopped when I reached out a hand to help him up.

He looked me over before taking my hand, and I did the same to him.

The boy was smaller than me but with a large oblong head reminding me of a fist. His eyes were set wide apart, and he had a flattened nose above thin lips. His hair was combed from one side across the top in wispy strands. He didn't strike me then as the kind of kid who'd ever be on the cover of *Boys' Life*, let's say.

"You got a library card for those?" I asked, nodding toward the books he'd dropped.

He glanced back. "No. I mean yes, I have permission from Reverend Pritchett to borrow whatever books I'd like."

His voice, louder than it needed to be, reminded me of the out-of-tune piano in the old church basement where we used to hold our Scout meetings back in Flushing, hollow and warbling.

He clasped my hand, and I helped him to his feet.

"Is that why you sneak inside?" I said.

He brushed wet leaves from the seat of his pants. "Well, it's hardly sneaking when the whole town knows you're allowed to do it."

"What's your name?" I asked.

He looked at me suspiciously. "What's yours?"

"Bud Castillo. My folks and I just—"

"You're the new people," he said, now less suspicious. "The diving man and his family."

"Yeah, that's us."

He tugged his shirt flat against his chest and said, "I'm Aubrey Marsh."

"As in Marsh Street?"

He sighed. "And Marsh Common and the Obed Marsh statue and the old Marsh Refinery. My family has lived here a long time," he said. "Well, not my family, the ones I live with, but the general one."

I pointed toward his stack of books. "What'd you get?"

"Oh," he said, turning the books around in his hands as though he had to check what they were. "*Meditations* by Marcus Aurelius, a little Ovid, some history, and *A Catalogue of the Manifold Variety of Winged Birds in the Massachusetts Colony.*"

"Are you studying for something?"

He shrugged. "Being a human, I guess."

You have to be careful about choosing the guys you ask about Scouting; back in Flushing, you could get made fun of pretty quick, if not shoved or punched in the shoulder, when you showed an interest in things like that. But from the start, I had a feeling Aubrey was someone like me – a lover of handbooks who liked trying them out on the world.

"Do you have a Scout troop in town?"

He shook his head. "I don't even know what a Scout troop is."

"It's a bunch of guys who get together to learn about things like camping and hiking and knots and living in the woods and how to be a decent human being."

"I don't feel like I'd be good at that."

"Which part?"

"Any of it," he said sadly.

"Well, that's the point. You, me, and some other kids—"

"There are no other kids," he said.

"This whole town has only you?"

"And now you," he said.

"Well, it's a start," I said. "I can tell you what I know from my books and you can tell me what you know from yours, and maybe we can try them out."

He nodded with some enthusiasm.

"But first, I've got to ask: what the hell happened to this town?"

"Better to show you," he said, starting to walk toward the street.

"What about my bike? Won't somebody steal it?"

Aubrey looked at me like I was insane. "Who around here can ride it?"

Together we walked a tour of Innsmouth, past his pointy-gabled stone house on Washington Street with boarded windows on one room in the corner, then through a district that used to be used for shipbuilding where a deep canal led to the Manuxet, and finally out to the docks which extended broken and rotten into the muck of the bay. In the distance past the breakwater, the rig stood atop a barge on choppy waters.

"It got here three days ago. They've been waiting for your father to help them lower those legs to the reef," Aubrey explained.

"Looks almost close enough to swim to," I said, thinking of the One Mile Swim badge I'd earned at Camp Flying Eagle.

"You wouldn't want to. That water is colder and rougher than it looks, and when you're out there, it's hard to tell which way is the shore."

"Have you done it?"

He shook his head. "I've heard talk."

We stopped afterward at the First National Grocery for some penny candy, and I was taken aback by Aubrey's zeal for sugary things. He grabbed a handful for both of us, placed it on "the Colonel's" tab, and then ate two-thirds of it himself before I could get any. We sat on the edge of the river with our legs dangling from the concrete bulwark.

"So when are we going to see it?"

"See what?" Aubrey asked.

"You said you'd show me what happened to town."

"I did," he said. "It died thirty years ago and now some of us are trying to bring it back to life."

I nodded in the direction of one of the many collapsing houses. "That doesn't look like it died of natural causes."

Aubrey considered and then said, "Nobody talks about it much. They call it 'the Unpleasantness,' and there isn't anybody still here from when it happened. I think it might have been a sickness that took them all, and the government destroyed the town to stop it from spreading."

It seemed incredible to me in 1963 when I was thirteen that the government could do such a thing, but I'd learn better soon.

"Where did all the people here now come from?"

"Reverend Pritchett found them, pretty much one or two at a time, all the kin of the old residents. He sent a telegram to my parents in Romania, begging them to bring back the Marsh name to the town their ancestors founded. I'd just been born, and they wanted me most of all. Something about the new generation."

"You're not an American?"

His back stiffened. "Of course I'm an American. My father was born here but met my mother over there."

"Was he in the war?"

"Everybody was in the war."

A terrible thought occurred to me, something that might disqualify Aubrey from being a Scout, at least in a troop anywhere near my father.

"What side did he fight on?"

"He fought for the Romanians, of course. Until he couldn't."

The discussion ended there, and we walked back to the library so I could get my bicycle. It was waiting for me just where I'd left it.

As I wheeled it out, Aubrey asked, "So if I wanted to be a Scout, how would I do it?"

"Well, we'd have meetings and you'd read the handbook, and maybe my dad would sign off on badges we'd earn."

"You have badges? And a book?" he asked with a quiet awe.

"Yeah. It's got everything you need to know. Come by my house tomorrow and I'll let you borrow it."

And that's how Aubrey Marsh became a Scout.

5

That night, ninety-five percent of our dinner conversation was about Dad's first day at work, and I waited (courteously, as the handbook would insist) for five percent to talk about my new friend and our new Scout troop.

My father had this strange way of telling the difference in his heart between people who were deliberate, arrogant idiots and people who were humble and accidental ones. He'd placed the dozen coworkers at the Innsmouth Oil Speculating Company into the latter category, and he even seemed to admire them more for what they didn't know than what they did.

"It's like they ordered this thing in the mail," he told us. "Which basically they did. It took three months to tow it from Venezuela, and it's in rough shape. Built for shallow water exploration, where you float it and then drop the legs. They call it the Maracaibo Explorer because that's the name on the side."

"Is it legitimate?" Mom asked. "Do they really think there's oil?"

Dad finished a bite of his pork chop. "They're damned motivated for sure. I'm the youngest guy there by twenty years or more, but they work hard and think what I say is gospel, which is nice for a change."

Explaining his high esteem for them.

"It's like they think if they believe hard enough, the oil will be there. The preacher comes out there every day too, checking on things and praying."

"Praying?"

Dad shook his head. "Don't ask me. He faces out to the sea with his arms open and yells something at the wind. He's basically their mayor, so he's got to make a big show of, you know, being optimistic or whatever."

"Speaking of optimistic—" I said, starting a segue I hadn't quite worked out in my mind.

"Has he said what religion he is?" Mom asked.

Dad scratched against his plate with his fork. "That church he's got has 'evangelical' in the name, so maybe it's one of those like they've got in the south where they yell and handle snakes."

My father didn't have a lot of interest in religion, though he'd been raised Catholic by my Puerto Rican grandparents after they emigrated to Brooklyn. The story was that they were alarmed my mother was Jewish when he introduced her to them, and he'd taken her hand and left their house never to speak to them again. Her folks hadn't been much more enthusiastic, and my dad used to say, "If God's got time to give a shit who marries who, which explains why this world is so screwed."

"We should go," Mom said. "As part of the community."

My father looked up at her, but before he could say anything, I took my moment.

"I met a kid today."

"Really?" my father said, surprised. "Who is he?"

I swear to God, that's when someone knocked on the lower

half of our front door. For years, Mom wouldn't believe I hadn't left him waiting outside.

Dad scowled. "Who the hell could that be?"

I was already on my feet because I knew who it had to be. I grabbed my handbook because I had a good idea what he wanted, too.

I opened the door and Aubrey stood on the front step, wearing a little vest and trousers like he'd been invited to dinner. I would later discover that's how he dressed for the evening.

When Mom arrived by my side, Aubrey took a deep bow with one hand to his stomach. "Good evening, Mrs. Castillo," he said.

Mom let out a single quick laugh but then recovered. "And also to you, young sir."

"This is Aubrey Marsh," I said. "I met him today at the library."

"Marsh?" I heard the squeak of my father's chair as he stood up. "As in Marsh Street? Marsh Refinery?"

"Yes, sir," Aubrey said. "Named for my ancestors, not for my family. We're what you might call the black sheep of the family."

My father arched his eyebrow. If there was one kind of person he liked, it was a black sheep.

"Would you like to come in?" Mom asked. "We still have some supper."

"No, thank you, Mrs. Castillo. I'm here to borrow a book."

I held out the Scout handbook and he took it from me in both hands with slow reverence.

"This has all of it?"

"Hiking, camping, citizenship...it's all there."

"And after I read it, I'll be..." He struggled for a word. "...a Scout?"

"Well," I said, deciding this was a good time to raise my idea with my dad less likely to say no in front of a stranger. "That all depends on whether we can get a Scoutmaster."

Aubrey looked over to my father.

"Me?" Dad asked. "I've never been a Scout in my life."

"You don't have to be," I said. I'd done a little research. "It says in the handbook that boys in remote places can form small troops with their dads."

"I don't know when I'd have time. I'm going to be leaving early and coming home late, and I'll need all the sleep I can get."

I suppose I should have seen it coming; Dad wasn't a joiner, especially for something he saw as "hokey" like the Scouts.

Aubrey rubbed his chin thoughtfully. "Does the handbook say 'father' exactly?"

It probably did, but I could see where he was going. "No, I don't think it does."

"Perhaps, Mrs. Castillo, you could serve instead," Aubrey suggested.

Mom told me later she was more honored by that request than many others in her life, and it always bothered me that I hadn't thought of it first.

"I...don't spend a lot of time outdoors," she told Aubrey.

"Neither does my mother. Your duties can be ceremonial."

"Ceremonial?"

"Bud and I can follow the rites in the manual—"

"They're just tips," I corrected.

"—and you can approve our progress."

Mom glanced from me to Dad and back to Aubrey, this strange little boy who'd fallen into our lives about five minutes earlier. I had a feeling she was weighing in her mind how bad it would be to disappoint the kid whose family had built the town.

"What else am I doing?" she said, with a sad smile I only understood much later. "I'll do it. Ceremonially."

Aubrey accepted with a nod. Then he held up the handbook. "I'll read this tonight."

"There's no hurry," I said.

What I didn't know was Aubrey had far fewer days left of being a boy than I did.

6

Aubrey changed everything, though not all at once.

He showed up at my house for our first (and only) formal patrol meeting on the Fourth of July wearing a pair of khaki pants and an olive-green buttoned shirt, the closest he could scrounge for a uniform. His mother had pinned the sleeves and pant cuffs to match the length of his spindly arms and legs. It looked too warm for summer, but now that I think about it, I never saw Aubrey sweat.

When he came in, Mom sat up from her drafting table and waved him over to admire his ingenuity. Then she motioned for him to turn slowly, which he did with some pride.

"All you need is one of those kerchiefs for your neck," she said.

He nodded. "We didn't have anything like that around the house."

"Well, here," Mom said, untying the red gingham one in her hair. "Take this."

"I couldn't—"

I took it instead and tied it under his collar.

"Now you look like a real Scout," Mom said, turning back to

her illustration for *Redbook,* one of her oldest clients, of a woman in a green dress smiling beside her new Frigidaire. They'd been the ones who responded when she said she was ready to work again.

Aubrey watched her a moment and then asked, "Is it for a book or a museum?"

"It's an ad for a magazine," Mom said.

"What is it selling?" he asked.

Mom laughed in a big cloud of cigarette smoke. "America," she said, bending closer again to the painting.

"Perfect," he said, holding up the triangular package he'd tucked under his arm. "I brought this for our Fourth of July flag raising. I borrowed it from the old Seaman's Bank Trust building."

"Did you?" she said. "I suppose we'd better find a place to raise it."

The three of us solemnly walked outside, which is when I realized we had no flagpole or even a bracket for one on our property. Luckily, we did have enough rope to throw over an elm branch, and with some tent pegs to keep it taut, we managed to raise Old Glory. I showed Aubrey how to do the Scout salute with his three center fingers, but he had a hard time bending in his thumb and pinky.

Mom watched us with her hand on her heart and her cigarette pinched in her lips, but when the flag reached the top, she was squinting as though to see it more clearly.

"How many stars is that?" she asked.

Aubrey glanced up, not long enough to count. "48. One for every state."

"There's fifty states, Aubrey," I said.

Mom chuckled.

"What did they add? The Philippines? Cuba?"

"Alaska and Hawaii," I said.

"Really?" He looked pained. "We'd better take it down."

"No," Mom said quickly. "I like it. What did Alaska or Hawaii ever do for us?"

We swore Aubrey in with a recitation of the Scout oath and the Scout Law, both of which he'd already memorized, and that first Scout meeting just stretched across the hazy summer all the way to September. Aubrey walked over most mornings after breakfast and went home some evenings before dinner and some after, if Mom was cooking meatloaf or pork chops he could slather with ketchup (which he'd never had and loved). Sometimes he'd stay the night, especially when he fell asleep on my dad's living room chair after we ate. Mom would pull a blanket over him as he snored in his loud gurgling way, and my father once said, "Aw. You don't know whether to tuck him in or throw him a fish."

I'll always remember that as the Summer of Aubrey, days and nights of trying to keep up with his almost desperate enthusiasm for Scouting. He was astonished that someone had written a whole book describing so clearly how to be a boy, and he accepted every word with the trust of someone who'd never seen how people treat each other in the world. Just like I had.

"People from Away must be really good," he said in wonderment.

"Well, not all," I'd try to tell him, but he didn't care.

He built a camp stove out of coffee cans. He wrote a comprehensive evacuation plan for the town in case of Soviet invasion, though we had to explain how the Soviets became the bad guys. He sewed his own sleeping bag out of a 19th-century quilt and stuffed it with duck feathers. He knew more knots than any sailor from *Treasure Island,* including some I think he made up like the "quadruple wolf-claw shank-hitch."

One time, Dad had swung his legs out of the Volkswagen bus after coming home from work when Aubrey came crashing through a hedge, clutching his left arm tied with a perfect tourniquet. Small as he was, he could be sneaky by accident that way.

"Jesus Christ!" Dad cried, jumping down. "What happened?"

Below the bandage, Aubrey's skin was paler even than normal. Above it, his flesh bulged purple. "First Aid!" he replied. "For the merit badge!"

When we weren't pitching tents in the backyard or tracking neighborhood wildlife, we'd walk downtown looking to do Good Turns. A Scout is supposed to do at least one Good Turn a day, something unplanned to help someone out. The classic example is helping an old lady cross the street with groceries, but you can save lost children, run errands for a shut-in, change a tire, whatever. The people of Innsmouth had plenty for us to do.

Once, we bandaged Mrs. Pym's bleeding elbow after she fell at the First National Grocery. Another time, we pulled the heavy vines off Mr. Carwin's family grave in Redemption Cemetery. We helped Dr. Brunner by cleaning the gutters around his office, requiring ladders and heavy gloves. We got a wasp's nest out of the Spivey sisters' mailbox, though Aubrey fled for his life from the swarm after we knocked it free.

We developed a sort of minor celebrity among the residents of town, and I'll admit I had my suspicions that people were saving up things for us to do just so we'd stop by. Everybody adored Aubrey, and it was a rare afternoon when we didn't get invited inside for bad raisin cookies and a drink of squeezed socks called Moxie.

What? We weren't in it for the rewards, so it's okay to be honest about them. A Scout is trustworthy, right?

Miss Delacroix is a good example. She waved us into her house one afternoon and asked us to carry her bedroom furniture downstairs.

"I won't be able to climb the steps much longer, and sleeping in my chair just won't do," she told us.

I'm not sure why she'd ask a four-foot-tall limping boy and another so thin you could clean a rifle with him to do that, but maybe we were just the handiest around. Her furniture weighed a ton, of course, but a Scout is helpful.

Like many of the houses I'd seen in Innsmouth, the inside of Miss Delacroix's had become a time machine, loaded with all the things she couldn't let go over the decades. Like most of the others, hers seemed to be locked into one decade, the Twenties, like she'd decided to live forever in the era she last understood.

There was a photo of a man in uniform on top of the dresser in her room, and when I peered closer at it, I noticed he had more than a little resemblance to Aubrey. Not like they were related, exactly, but like they had come from the same place: their wide-set eyes with narrow lids, their flat-ish noses, even their wispy hair made it hard not to ask who he was.

"Is that your son?" I asked, like a total idiot.

Miss Delacroix laughed and laughed, but then finally said, "No, he was my fiancé many, many years ago. I guess he hasn't aged in there like I have out here."

"He looks a little like—" I glanced at Aubrey, who was gathering pillows from the bed.

"—people around here used to," Miss Delacroix supplied, nodding.

My mom would have scowled at me for my next question, but I had to know. "Where is he now?"

She held the picture closer to examine it and shook her head. "He married a woman with whom he had...more in common."

I must have made a face of regret or embarrassment because she reached for my arm. "Oh, no, it was a long time ago and we were both so stupid."

Yet here she had his picture on her dresser like she was still waiting for him to pick her up for a dance that ended half a century earlier. "Miss" Delacroix had kept her name by never marrying, staying free in case he ever came back, and he deserved an ass-kicking, not a place of honor. Or so it seemed to a thirteen-year-old kid.

"A guy who could do something like that to a girl doesn't belong on anyone's dresser," I said quietly.

She pulled me close with a shaking arm on my shoulder. "I appreciate you saying so, but I couldn't follow where he was going. Not then. And if I could, I'd never have gone west and never reported for Mr. Hearst's newspapers and never got to see as much as I did."

"You were a reporter?"

"I was a newswoman," Miss Delacroix said with dignity.

"One of the first at the scene of the Black Dahlia murder."

"What was that?"

There's a window in a kid's age for adults where they feel obligated to protect us, but if you catch them when they're younger or older, they'll pretty much tell you anything. Which is how we spent an afternoon reading through Miss Delacroix's scrapbooks, gorging ourselves on cookies, and moving one piece of oaken furniture downstairs about every forty-five minutes. It was the best afternoon with an old person I'd ever had, though a little sad.

She wanted to be in Innsmouth, even if it was crumbled... maybe because it was. She felt like she'd missed something, even the bad parts.

A lot of those folks had stories like hers. They'd almost all lit out from town to make their fortunes sometime in the mid-Twenties. Mr. Pym jumped a boxcar and rode out to California. The Spivey sisters joined a circus as a trapeze act. Mr. Harben the pharmacist had been a part of the Carter-Carnarvon expedition to King Tutankhamun's tomb. Others had been sailors or soldiers, railroad men or workers for the Tennessee Valley Authority. Yet in the end, they'd all come back.

I asked Aubrey once if he thought that was strange, and all he said was, "You can't help where your home is."

7

Scout's first hike is his introduction to a world of adventure, at least according to the handbook, and Aubrey planned his with maps borrowed from town hall and our route measured out to scale with a protractor. He had a clear idea of where he wanted to go, and I was fine with taking his lead – though maybe I should have been a little more suspicious, looking back on it.

The only picture Mom ever took of me and Aubrey was on the day of the hike, and though it's long gone, I can describe it from memory.

There are two boys standing in front of a pale gray Victorian porch, one taller than the other. Both are squinting in the glare of a slightly cloudy New England summer morning, and the taller one on the left holds his hand to his brow like a visor.

The smaller boy looks like he just parachuted behind enemy lines at Normandy. He's wearing a comically enormous field pack with a flashlight clipped to the left shoulder strap and a tin cup hanging from the right. He's wearing a khaki shirt and shorts, and thick socks droop over the tops of his hiking boots. He has his hands on his hips and his mouth is open because he's saying, "Daylight's wasting, Mrs. Castillo!"

To which my mother replied, "It's 1/50th of a second, Aubrey." Then, turning to business, she asked, "What's the plan?"

"Four miles out and four miles back," Aubrey said.

"Lunch?"

I pointed to Aubrey's pack. "Cheese sandwiches, a box of crackers, and two sodas." There was also half of a pie, but I didn't think that was worth mentioning.

"Water?"

"Right here," Aubrey said, tapping the sloshing canteen clipped to his belt.

"What time should I assume you're dead if you're not home?"

"Nightfall," Aubrey said.

"Excellent. Wish I could go with you, but commerce stops for no woman." She kissed the top of my head and squeezed Aubrey close by the shoulder. He'd gone from flinching at that kind of thing to leaning into it like a cat. "Go west, young men!"

That's what we did, clanking first down my street and then onto the wider road toward the edge of town. There, we jumped a fence beside the old red brick railroad depot and started down the abandoned tracks toward a town called Rowley. The handbook advises against walking near tracks, but it was clear from the plumes of yellowed grass between the ties that these hadn't seen a locomotive in decades.

The ties had rotten hollow, and our steps sounded thock-crunch, thock-crunch as we went from wood to gravel and back to wood again. Not that there was anything out among those bushes and spindly trees to hear it; aside from a few birds, we didn't see anything alive.

I'd packed lighter than Aubrey, but I did bring along my portable radio in case the conversation flagged. With Aubrey it seldom did, but for reasons I wouldn't learn until later, he wasn't in a mood much to talk yet that morning. So I played the hits from WRKO warbling their way from Boston, everything from the Everly Brothers to the Kingsmen.

It wasn't until after "Tell Laura I Love Her" when Aubrey spoke up.

"So the guy crashes his motorcar to show Laura he loves her?"

"Well, it wasn't on purpose," I said. "He was racing."

"Laura's lucky if you ask me."

"How do you figure?"

"What kind of husband or father would that idiot have been even if he won the race? A gentleman with a future would have written her a politely worded note with a fountain pen on some nice linen paper."

"Is that what you'd have done?"

"Well, if there wasn't a family heirloom ring to give, I'd tell her the truth: I don't have enough money to get her the kind of ring society thinks I should. Why set up an expectation I might not be able to fill later on?"

"Oh, Aubrey," I said, clutching my hand to my heart. "Take me home and love me forever!"

By the two-mile mark out of town, the tracks had entered thick woods, with trees looming too close to the rails for a train to pass through. The shadows from them grew even longer as the clouds darkened with approaching rain.

"We might need to wrap this up sooner than we thought," I said.

"We're only a quarter of the way," Aubrey replied, pointing ahead.

"The weather's about to turn," I said.

"What's a little weather to Scouts?"

Aubrey, who'd spent most of his life living in an attic by the look of him, had never been caught in a storm, his hiking boots heavy and sloshing with rain, a poncho sticking to his back and arms like a giant dead bat.

Who was I to deny him that?

A breeze picked up and the trees seemed to awaken from their stillness, which is always my favorite part of the storm. Aubrey's too, judging by him turning his face straight up to the sky for the first large drops to hit his cheek.

We reached into our packs for the dead bat ponchos and got them over our heads while the rain was still only surging down in bursts. Then came the waves of it with every gust, and soon I was bolting after Aubrey as he ran further down the tracks.

He paused at a break in the trees, and I could tell by a wooden post that there had once been a sign or marker there. He pointed, said something I couldn't hear, and then pushed his way through the narrow path.

"Wait!" I yelled after him, but he'd already been swallowed by the foliage and all I could do was go after him.

After a hundred yards or so, we emerged into a wide field, and standing at its far edge was a two-story brick building with its windows boarded tightly shut. It had the look of a military barracks, something built for use and not for show, though the sheltered porch on the front of the building still had a few half-rotten rocking chairs on it.

We ran onto the porch and skidded to a stop near a set of double doors that were crossed by steel beams held in place by massive bolts.

"What is this place, Aubrey?" I said between gasps for air.

Aubrey, coughing from the damp with his hands on his knees, didn't answer.

"Did you know this was here?" I asked, patting him on the back to loosen whatever was stuck.

He nodded now, swallowing. "I'd heard about it."

I peeled a loose board aside from one of the windows and squinted inside at an empty room.

"Did you hear about what's inside?"

Aubrey took out a short pry bar from his pack. "Want to find out?"

The handbook says to seek shelter from a storm and leave a place better than you found it, so I figured we could pick up some trash inside and call it even.

Aubrey handed me the pry bar and I popped the half dozen boards off of the window frame nearest the door. I tugged at the window assuming it was locked, but on the third try, it creaked upward.

Aubrey had already unclipped his flashlight, the military kind bent into an L shape.

"I've got all the colored signal lenses for it, too," he said proudly.

I clasped my hands to form a step for him to climb inside. I followed right after, and we found ourselves in a lobby with a reception desk and chairs. Everything was coated in dust, and our damp feet were turning the tiled floor to mud.

This being the center of the building, hallways of the same length extended on either side of where we stood. Someone had tried to barricade the left one with a tangle of chairs from the waiting area.

I heard the creak of a wooden drawer and turned quickly to see Aubrey searching the desk.

"What are you looking for?"

"Evidence." He held up a notepad with a letterhead reading Naval Medical Research Institute, Bethesda MD.

"Why would the Navy be here?"

Aubrey didn't answer, stepping down the corridor of pale green tile to the right. On both sides were a series of doors. We opened each and they seemed to be examination rooms, none of them with a complete set of furniture: one had an examination table, another a counter, a third a spinning stool. All of them had deep bathtubs.

"A hospital," I whispered, though I didn't know why.

Aubrey nodded.

On our left, we arrived at a massive room with two sets of doors at either end, and inside was the largest swimming pool I'd ever seen, far wider and deeper than the one at Camp Flying Eagle. One side was thick glass, and a narrow walkway descended along it so people could observe what was going on under the surface. Something as large as a cow floated in the pale green muck, but it was covered by a tarp.

Aubrey found a metal pole far taller than he was, and it spun crazily as he approached the edge.

"No way," I said, grabbing one end.

"What if it's a body?"

"Exactly," I said.

He tugged the pole from my grasp, and I'll admit I didn't try hard to hold on. He balanced it carefully, leaning over the goop, and I wondered how long he'd be under before I'd have a chance to grab him. A good ten seconds for sure.

The pole wobbled closer and closer to the mass, and it made contact with a thump. Whatever it was listlessly rotated with a loud gurgle of bubbles. Aubrey screamed and dropped the pole, and I grabbed him by the pack so he wouldn't fall in.

We watched the pole disappear into the water and faintly heard it clunk against the glass.

"Probably just trash," I said, hoping it was true.

We left that room and headed for the end of the corridor. There we came to a set of stairs, jammed with toppled filing cabinets like someone had been trying to push them down to the ground floor. Some had opened and tossed out their papers.

Aubrey stooped, picked one up, and skimmed it.

"Medical chart," he said. He grabbed three or four others and stuffed them in his backpack.

"Isn't that stealing?"

He looked up at me with a confused expression. "From whom?"

He stood and then started back the other way. When we got to the lobby, he nudged past the chairs and kept going until I grasped his elbow.

"Where are you going?"

"To the other set of stairs," he said. "There's one at each end."

"Why?"

"To see what's on the second floor."

I wasn't scared, exactly, though I had a strong sensation of being unwelcome. It wasn't a ghostly thing but more of a New York one: there wasn't such a thing as a truly abandoned building back in Queens, and I'd been chased by plenty of old rummies out of their "homes."

"It's just more of the same, don't you think?"

He shrugged. "One way to find out," he said, going up the stairs.

The second floor was in worse condition than the first. Soot streaked the walls and burnt furniture lay in pieces. Some of the windows had shattered, but the glass hadn't fallen inside but out. Chips gouged in the walls looked like the marks I'd imagine bullets might make.

"What happened here?" I asked.

"Something bad," Aubrey said quietly.

He looked into one room that must have been a surgery with a steel table tipped on its side. In the next was something like a dentist's chair, and we didn't stay in there long. Both rooms had prominent drains in the center of the floor, as though the builders had expected a lot of liquid.

Aubrey's pace quickened and he was throwing open doors, glancing inside, and then moving on to the next.

"Hey, what are you looking for?"

He wasn't listening. He slammed himself against a jammed door once and then twice before it gave way, and by then I caught up to him and grabbed him so roughly by the shoulders that he let out a yelp. I let go, but I was still angry.

"Why did you bring me here?"

His face was wet with more than the rain, and he said in a pained voice, "They never told me."

The room we'd fallen into seemed to be an administrator's office, and Aubrey began yanking open cabinets and drawers again, letting books and files slide to the floor and only glancing at them as they fell. Sometimes he'd pick one up and then shove it in his pack.

"Aubrey!" I had to yell for him even to hear me. "What are we doing here?"

"Grab as much as you can," he said.

I was about to seize his arm again when I stopped myself, remembering the last time I'd done that to someone in Queens. Then I heard another reason to stop.

Somewhere below us, we heard the unmistakable sound of a door closing and we both froze. I was about to say it had to be the wind, but then a second one closed.

No building is ever really abandoned, even in Innsmouth.

Aubrey opened his mouth to speak but I raised my finger to my lips. Then I pointed at the hallway, and he crept out of the office. Footsteps echoed from the unblocked stairwell we'd used to get up here, which meant we couldn't go down that way.

I waved Aubrey to follow me, and we hurried to the other end of the floor where the filing cabinets were clogging the stairs. By then, the footsteps had reached the opposite end of the hallway, but it was too dark to see who it was...or for them to see us.

There was only one thing to do, so I counted off to ten and then jumped with both feet onto the top filing cabinet. It made a squeal against the wall and then stopped. I waved Aubrey to jump, and when he did, his added weight was enough to send the entire mass screeching and clanging down to the first floor with us stumbling behind it. I'll never know how neither of us twisted an ankle.

We ran for our entrance window, climbed through, and then ran back for the tracks as quickly as we could, our ponchos flapping behind us.

If anyone followed, he wasn't as fast as we were.

8

Maybe this isn't kind to say, but Aubrey would never have been a model for Rockwell's paintings in the Scout handbook, at least physically. I wouldn't either, as skinny as I was, but Aubrey added short stature and the kind of puffy pale skin you get after falling asleep in a bathtub to his disqualifying factors, not to mention the strange gurgle he made when he breathed.

So I wasn't surprised he got sick after our hike. On the way back to town, he was already coughing and shivering pretty violently, and as soon as Mom saw us on the porch, she came out to swaddle him in towels. We got him into the Volkswagen and took him home, but when we got him to the door, he wouldn't let us help him inside.

"My parents...startle easily," he managed to say through chattering teeth.

"I've got to explain to your mother what happened," Mom said. "This is all my fault."

"No, it's not," he said. "She knows that."

He opened the door with a little brass skeleton key from a chain on his neck, but only enough to slip through. I tried to catch a glimpse of the house, but it was dark with a flickering light somewhere deeper inside.

All the way home, Mom kept saying, "They'll never let him near us again."

I'll admit I wasn't sure myself, and I guess Dad wasn't either. That night when he leaned into my room to check on me, he said, "Hey, be careful with the kid, okay? He's a lot more fragile than those chuckleheads back in Queens, and I'd hate to lose my job because you killed the boy whose name is on half the town."

More fragile. That kept me awake thinking, for sure. Jaime and Frank had been fragile enough when I went ape at the Scout meeting, which I'd never risk for Aubrey. It's one thing to be a little crazy like my dad, but it's another to hurt other people with it.

But then, he's the one who brought me to that hospital.

Mom sent an apology to the Marshes on her best stationery the next morning, and the reply came back in a thin, shaky handwriting assuring us that our quick thinking made the situation much better than it could have been, and Aubrey isn't always conscious of his limitations. It was signed, "Mrs. Sorina Marsh."

"Such a pretty name," Mom said.

It took Aubrey four days to recover enough to visit again. When he entered our house, you'd think he came back from a war overseas. Mom stood up from her drafting table and held him by the shoulders to look him over.

"Are you feeling all right?"

"Yes, Mrs. Castillo," Aubrey said, trying to sound modest though I knew he was enjoying the attention. "I just have to be careful about moisture."

"Moisture," I said.

"Yes." He dusted himself off for no reason. "So is it time for another meeting?"

"It sure is," I said, leading him upstairs to the Scout den we'd fashioned out of one of the many empty bedrooms, complete with the board of sample knots, a big wooden spool as a table, a deck of cards, and a bunch of old issues of *Boys' Life* and *National Geographic*. Aubrey sure loved a good map.

I closed the door behind us, and he turned with a quizzical look on his face.

"A Scout is trustworthy, right?" I demanded.

He nodded.

"And loyal? Scouts are loyal?"

His eyes narrowed as much as they could and his smile faded. "I didn't tell you about where we were going, and I'm sorry."

"You're sorry. Why didn't you tell me?"

"I was afraid you wouldn't want to go."

"Why did you want to go?"

He sat down at the end of a green velvet thing my mother had called a settee. "I had heard it was out there and nobody ever went and I thought it had something to do with...what happened. The Unpleasantness."

"You might be on to something," I said, maybe a little hysterically. "We sure got to see some Unpleasantness."

I'm not proud of how I treated Aubrey that day, but the truth is I was scared not just of the place but of him. Of what he knew and wasn't saying.

He didn't catch my sarcasm. "It was a sickness, I was right about that."

"You ran through there like you knew what you were looking for."

"I didn't know exactly," he said, opening the satchel he'd brought with him. "But I had an idea what I'd find. Look at these."

He handed me some of the files he'd grabbed from the floor. Mostly they were scraps, a form here or a set of notes there. I wasn't paying attention as I flipped through them.

"Look at the names."

When I did, I saw some familiar ones: a Thaddeus Pym, a Philip Spivey, a Helen Olmstead. All last names for current residents in Innsmouth.

"So they're family of the people in town? The ones they left behind?"

"Yes. Can you imagine? You go away and hear maybe months or even years later that everybody you cared about died in an epidemic while you escaped."

"We don't know they died. They might have cured it, at least for some of the people." The instant I said it, I knew it didn't wash and Aubrey explained why.

"Would the place look like that if they were cured?"

The room had gotten dark, not from anything as dramatic as a thunderstorm but from the typical cloud cover that arrived most summer days. Neither of us turned on a light.

"No," I said. "It would look like that if they were quarantined and could never get out."

"They probably caught the disease from one of the ships, coming back from some faraway place. It spread too fast to even tell relatives—"

"—and then the Navy arrived to investigate because the disease was carried over the sea."

It made a weak kind of sense, but something was still missing.

"But if their loved ones died, why come back when Pritchett asked them? All their family was dead or long gone. What would be the point?"

Aubrey shook his head. "Probably not to rebuild a town."

I thought about my dad, who at that moment was somewhere deep in Innsmouth Harbor breathing through a hose and groping around a field of shattered stone. "Or to drill for oil."

Aubrey didn't say anything, just stared at the worn circular rug that was probably owned by a person who'd died in that hospital or this town or maybe even this room.

I sat next to him. "Hey, if we're going to be Scouts together, friends, I've got to know everything you do about this. You can't hold anything back, okay?"

He nodded, still not looking up.

"Something isn't right here, but if I'm square with you and you're square with me, we may have a chance to figure it out."

"Yeah," he said. Then, more strongly, "Yeah."

"Is there anything else left that you know and I don't?"

He nodded to the file still in my hand. "Look at the symptoms."

I glanced down at a page of notes, handwritten and signed by a Dr. Samuel Charbonneau, USN. I skimmed the page not knowing what he was getting at: raw and flaking skin, pulmonary edema, chills, aquaphilia...whatever that was.

"I have what they had," Aubrey said.

I laughed because I couldn't help it. "How could you? They were all dead decades before you came here."

"What if it isn't something you catch but something you're… born with?"

"Aubrey, if that were true then your mom or dad would have it."

"Mother is nervous about the sun and talking to people, and she looks a lot like me."

"What's wrong with that? She's your mother. And if she had this disease, she'd be dead by now."

"All I know is I'm not like you or like the boys in the Scout handbook."

"Nobody is like the boys in the handbook. The guys I knew back in Flushing all had zits and crooked teeth and hair cut by their mothers. They stank from their armpits. The artist didn't draw that in the handbook. You see me in there? Not a lot of half Puerto Rican, half Jews on those pages."

"I'm not like you, either," Aubrey said.

"What are you talking about? You're better than me. You know a lot more and you think like an adult and you see stuff I'd never notice. You're going to live longer than I will, not being an idiot and all."

"But if I have the sickness—"

"Gimme that canteen out of your bag," I said.

He seemed confused, so I grabbed it myself. Then I twisted off the cap, tipped it to my lips, and made a big show of sloshing around a gulp of water in my mouth.

"Mmmm hmmm," I said. "That's some delicious sickness water! Can't wait to get the Innsmouth disease!"

Aubrey sat staring up at me, shocked and blinking.

"If you're dying, I'm dying," I said. "So we'd better hurry and figure out what's wrong with this town."

9

We'd managed to live two months in Innsmouth without going to the Evangelical Progress Temple, but our luck ran out not long after the hike.

Dad came home one night after another long day on the Maracaibo – they'd anchored the legs and he was diving now three times a day to scout the reef — and he found me and Mom reading in the parlor.

She looked up from the couch and I looked up from his chair, and he seemed annoyed.

"What's the matter?" Mom asked.

He held his hands on his hips and shook his head. "I held Pritchett off as long as I could, but if we don't show up at church this Sunday, he's going to think something's wrong with us."

"We could have just gone," Mom said. "What would it hurt?"

Of all the Scout laws, the one I learned least from home was Reverence. The handbook doesn't bang the God drum too hard, but it suggests going to church every Sunday and saying your prayers before bed. I'm not sure what you were even supposed to pray about because my folks never taught me.

Mom and Dad remembered their religions as the cause of arguments and disownings and two weeping mothers on the phone before they just went down to City Hall for the wedding in clothes they bought from Gimbels.

"That judge who did the marrying may not have been God," my dad liked to say, "but at least we could find him when we needed him."

We celebrated Christmas with a tree, mostly because everyone else around us did and we liked to trade presents, but I didn't know Easter from Yom Kippur. My parents seemed to have a vague belief that some conscious force was clumsily in charge of the universe, but it only came up when my father was yelling about how bad a job it was doing.

"The thing is," Dad said, "if we make an appearance now, they'll expect it again."

"Oh, Ted, come on. What does a couple of hours each Sunday matter? It'll make me feel less like we're robbing this town."

That's how we found ourselves three days later in our dress clothes — including the suit my father had been married in and me in a brown sport coat that was one long reach away from splitting under the arms. Mom, of course, had a sky-blue dress which turned out to be the brightest thing in that church.

The Evangelical Progress Temple, so labeled on the sign out front with the movable letters, had once been a Masonic lodge if the chipped carving above the door was anything to go by.

From the inside, it was much more impressive than St. Mary's back home. Twenty rows of pews faced a towering altar made of rough granite, more like something you'd see outdoors than in. Marble columns held a domed ceiling of painted navy-blue skies and gold speckled stars above us. Mosaic ceramic tiles formed an enormous star on the floor, overlaying an Earth thirty feet wide. Glass shone blue in the oceans. Long felt banners hung down from the rafters along the walls, embroidered with crosses, tridents, Stars of David, and crescents.

"I guess they've got all the bases covered," Dad muttered, and Mom shot him one of her famous still-smiling elbows to the ribs.

I saw Aubrey leaning from one side to the other trying to look around the edge of the crowd for us, and when he saw me wave, he hurried over with a dignified mustachioed man limping behind him. The man wore a gray suit with a single military medal pinned to the lapel.

"Mr. and Mrs. Castillo, may I present my father, Colonel Nathaniel Marsh," Aubrey announced, not quite reaching us yet. My parents turned, startled as always by his sudden presence and voice, but they recovered quickly.

Colonel Marsh bowed in the same way Aubrey had the day he met my parents, and he took my mother's hand. Then he shook my father's.

"Colonel," Dad said. "I'm Ted and this is Virginia."

"Aubrey has told me all about you both," said the Colonel in an accent mixing the flatness of New England with a trill to the ends of his R's and T's.

"Uh, oh." Dad glanced at Aubrey.

"Not at all. A soldier, like me." The Colonel tapped the medal on his chest. "A man who knows what things cost."

My father might have hugged him or at least gotten talking, but Aubrey held out his arm for my mother. "We'd better get seated and I'll tell you all about what's going on."

We took a pew about midway to the altar, Dad waiting for all of us to sit down before taking the end so he could bolt if he had to. Aubrey sat between Mom and I, and the Colonel sat beside my father.

"This isn't a traditional church," Aubrey explained to Mom.

"I'd gathered so," she said.

"Reverend Pritchett likes us to be more open-minded. He says God has many faces and many arms, reaching into all our lives."

That didn't sound appealing to me, and apparently not to my mother, who nodded unsmiling.

"Me, I believe more in the watchmaker God," Aubrey said, "something that started the world and is too busy doing other things most of the time to change anything every day. Or maybe it's a big experiment. Anyway, people here aren't too picky about what you believe as long as you believe in Innsmouth."

By then, most of the town had settled into their seats and Pritchett stepped out behind the altar in white robes, a gold sash, and something like the hat you'd see on the Pope.

"Modest and understated," my father mumbled.

Aubrey leaned across his father to whisper, "The Reverend's something of a performer."

And so he was. A choir of women from town, the Spivey sisters and Miss Delacroix among them, formed on each side and sang...something I couldn't make out. It wasn't in English and it wasn't in Latin because my father sat squinting at them.

"They practice a lot, but...you know," Aubrey said to Mom, shrugging.

Pritchett lifted his arms like a conductor and the congregation rose and began to sing the same hymn. An old organ wheezed from the corner with Dr. Brunner tickling the ivories, and the sound resonated with surprising strength against the marble walls.

I noticed the Colonel was singing but Aubrey was only humming. He didn't know the words any more than we did.

When the music ended and Pritchett lowered his arms, voices faded and there was a lot of echoed squeaking and scraping as people sat down again. He waited at the pulpit for everyone to settle, leaning and gazing off like a man lost in thought, about to improvise some great religious insight.

He turned to face us. "Y'all ever feel stuck Between?"

There was a definite capital-B in the way Pritchett said it. "Like when you're down in Town Square tryin' to remember if you went there for groceries or your medicine, so you're turnin' and turnin'?"

He shuffled around in a little circle and people laughed.

"That's being stuck Between. When you feel you're too young to be old and too old to be young, that's stuck Between, too. We spend our whole lives that way, don't we? I guess that's what living really is, the hours we spend between birth and death, waking and sleeping, back then and someday soon."

Some of the people in the pews were starting to nod in agreement, which was more motion than I'd ever seen at St. Mary's the few times we went at Christmas.

"We in Innsmouth, we know from Between, right? Land and sea, body and spirit, living and dead, here and somewhere else. It takes courage from the center of your heart to live Between, and it's exhausting, isn't it? Whew. You know it is. And not just for us. Lots of folks stuck Between in this world, like all those brothers and sisters down South tired of living Between free and slave, inside and outside. Can't blame them for wanting to know the score for sure one way or the other, even at the end of a billy club."

Pritchett blotted some beads of sweat from his forehead with a handkerchief.

"The simple people out there Away, they don't like Between. Why? Because they know the people who live like we do are better than they are, more evolved, able to stretch and bend with the world instead of breaking like they would. They hate the gray because they're weakest where we're strong."

Someone cried out "Amen!" in a warbling voice. Aubrey was leaning forward, rapt.

"But we won't be stuck Between forever, right? That gentleman back there is helping us." Pritchett pointed and my father's eyes went wide as everyone turned to face him and applaud. Dad raised a hand and smiled a little, which turned the applause into a cheer.

"Time's coming, my friends, when a choice will appear before you and you'll have to pick what you are. And instead of being scared, I want you to feel relieved. Excited. Ready. Joyous because the real you squirming inside these ill-fitting people suits will feel cool waters at last."

Dad glanced at Mom and then at me. I shrugged because I had no idea where this was going.

"What will your choice be?"

I thought the question was rhetorical, but then Pritchett pointed with great drama straight at me.

"Bud Castillo, will you choose New York or Innsmouth?"

"Uh, I'm—" I knew how I wanted to answer and how I should answer weren't the same thing, and so did he.

"That's okay, son. There's still time." He pointed at Miss Delacroix. "Ma'am, will you choose 1927 or 1963?"

"1963, through and through," she said, prompting some applause.

Pritchett motioned to Dr. Brunner. "Good sir, will you choose science or spirit?"

Hand on his chest, Brunner said, "I choose spirit."

Again another cheer. "Mrs. Virginia Castillo," Pritchett cried.

Mom looked up and squinted at him, not unlike a gunslinger.

"Will you choose artist or mother?"

"Both," she said.

Pritchett smiled. "You're going to surprise yourself when the time comes." He then turned a searing gaze at Aubrey.

"Young Aubrey Marsh, yours is the toughest choice of all." Pritchett let the crowd quiet down. "Will you be boy or man?"

The entire congregation turned in their pews to smile at Aubrey expectantly, like they were prompting him for the correct answer.

Mom, frowning, put her arm around him, but he sat up straight with his chin forward and said, "Man."

The parishioners burst into a cheer you'd expect more from a Mets game than a church service. They went wild, or at least as wild as they could at their ages: rising to their feet, holding their hands above their heads, looking heavenward with eyes closed in ecstasy.

Aubrey for his part looked slightly abashed. He smiled and

shrugged at me, but he accepted the attention without any sign of the terror I'd have felt for so many people to want something from me.

Pritchett was coming down the aisle now with his choir, the robes dragging behind him. "This boy, brothers and sisters, he's the start of a whole new life for all of us. Ted Castillo may be opening the way, but Aubrey Marsh...he'll be our first one through."

Through to what? If Aubrey knew, I couldn't see it in his expression of polite cluelessness.

"Dr. Brunner!" Pritchett turned toward the organ. "Play us the music of the new Innsmouth."

And he did. I'd never heard tones combined like that before and I haven't heard them since, not even in all the rest of the 60s when I heard sitars and theremins and guitars badly tuned, sometimes while taking distorting substances. No psychonaut or Aquarian could have imagined the abstract cacophony blasting from those organ pipes like the calls of whales.

Many of the others sang along, and their voices matched the pitch of the music like a single creature connected at the lungs.

People approached us, pumping my father's hands in thanks and kissing my mother's cheek and gripping my shoulders. They hugged Aubrey tight over and over, and I worried they'd smother him. The Colonel seemed less excited than everyone else, watching over his boy with a hand on his shoulder so no one could carry him away.

The congregation spilled out from the front doors of the temple, and outside it was bright even for summer. There were halos around everything alive, the kind you get when you swim too long with your eyes open, and I stumbled out in a random direction because I couldn't quite see.

There was a potluck afterward on tables with red-checkered cloths, steaming plates of fish and rice, not to mention two rows of pies. It took some doing to get even close to Aubrey with all the older folks doting on him, kissing his cheek, tousling his hair. Every time I approached, it seemed like another person was in the way, either excited to see him or excited to see me.

When I found him alone sitting on the steps of the temple with his tie hanging dangerously over some beans, I sat down beside him.

"Do you have any idea what—"

He shook his head. "None at all. There's never been a service like that one before."

"What do they mean you're going through first? Going through what?"

He looked up from his plate, frowning. "I think they mean I'm going to die."

"What? Who'd be excited about that? Besides, they said you'd be the first, which would have to mean everyone else would have to—"

"Boys!" Reverend Pritchett came over, grin on his face and a chicken leg in one hand. He sat between us. "That's what I call a service! Did you both feel the spirit in there?"

"Reverend," I said, "Where is Aubrey going 'through'?"

Pritchett and Aubrey both seemed surprised, the first amused and the other horrified.

The reverend said, "You're a direct young man, like your old man. It's a great quality, and it deserves directness in return.

Aubrey is going into the future, that's all — the future of Innsmouth. He's the first because he's the youngest, the ones most eager for the new. He's a special boy because he's both the last and the first of us."

"What's in that future?"

Pritchett raised a finger to his lips. "You'll see."

10

July gave way to August, and soon we had to figure out how I'd go to school. I was in no hurry, but Mom insisted she wouldn't have a feral son. With no single person in Innsmouth qualified to teach, Dr. Brunner devised the clever alternative of having Aubrey and I do daily rotations with subject experts in the town. That meant some odd gaps in our education – I learned accounting from Mr. Farkas before I knew algebra – but it beat sitting at a desk all day long. Aubrey joined me, though he was more advanced than me in most ways.

Miss Delacroix took on our English education, assigning us essays to write and books to read. These latter she chose from shelves of old paperbacks, starting with *In Cold Blood* which dragged a little much for a story with "blood" in the title. Next was *Of Mice and Men*, after which Aubrey sullenly decided he was Lenny and I was George.

"No way," I told him. "If anybody's a dangerous idiot petting a mouse in his pocket, it's me."

"You're not dangerous," he said, which wasn't as complete or comforting as he meant it to be.

We learned a clumsy kind of physics from Chief Lambert

and his volunteer firefighters, mostly how fun it was to knock over brick walls with high pressure firehouses. Constable Connaghan took us to shoot cans with a revolver so rusty I thought it would explode in our hands, which was the only thing I could do better than Aubrey. Harriet and Edith Spivey taught us how to embroider a sampler, and we were both terrible.

History was one subject nobody was willing to share, though we did manage to find out some more about the Unpleasantness from Mr. Pym when he came ashore to teach us some carpentry to build birdhouses.

"Well, the way I heard it," he told us, "was that some idiot from Away came strutting into town, researching his family roots. He got to poking around where he wasn't supposed to, asking a lot of questions, getting the wrong idea about things. People around here have always been a little different, but good different, you know? How many more big-eyed, pink-skinned money-grubbers do we need in the world?"

I didn't have an exact number, but I agreed it was lower than the current tally, for sure.

"They got a committee together to talk to him, set him straight, but then he got spooked and did a lot of damage to the old Gilman House trying to bust out. The whole town went tracking him down like a lost cat, but then he slipped off into the woods and back to Arkham or Boston or wherever."

"What happened to town, then?"

"Authorities came back, decided there was a sickness, and then called in the Navy to quarantine us. They built a hospital, people say, but I've never seen it."

Probably a good thing, I thought.

Dr. Brunner was the first to clue us in to how that sickness might work. It was his job to teach us biology, mostly evolution and genetics. I never quite got up the courage to ask Brunner where his accent came from, but he showed us tables with the brain masses of the races and how to measure their volume with sunflower seeds in plaster skull casts.

"Racism is a failure of imagination," he said. "All of life is a toolbox, and we are all the right tool for something. For example, you Master Castillo combine the canniness of the Jew with the passionate temper of the indigenous tribes of the islands."

I didn't dare tell my parents about that when I got home.

"Life is not designed for duplication but for improvement, one generation at a time. We mix and we mix, and some of the mixes are dead ends. Most don't go on, and the river of destiny passes them by. They have too much of something or not enough, and they fail to bloom."

"Is that what happened in Innsmouth? People failed to bloom?"

"What happened in Innsmouth, young man, is people from Away didn't know what blooming was," Brunner said, closing the subject for the day and the ones after.

On the way home that afternoon, I had a terrible thought and asked Aubrey about it.

"Do you think these people wish they were sick?"

He frowned. "If they do, it's only because they have the choice."

A week or two later, we had a chance to see firsthand some people from Away who didn't know what blooming was.

When Dad could make it home for dinner (rarely), Aubrey

was handy for his patience on adjusting the rabbit ears on our TV to catch a signal from somewhere civilized, sometimes Boston. One night while trying to get some old Western movie to fizzle onto the screen for my father, we saw pictures of a burned-out church in Birmingham instead.

"Oh, my God," said Mom.

"What happened?" Aubrey asked her, peering through the static.

She leaned closer with the rest of us, listening to Walter Cronkite describe the bombing by dynamite that had killed those four little girls in their church. People in the city had gone insane, it seemed, and now there were crowds fighting in the streets.

"Why would someone hurt them?" Aubrey asked, looking around at all of us, maybe a little scared we'd come from a society of barbarians. I was, too. I knew people weren't always good, but I'd never imagined they'd bomb a church.

"Because the world is full of jackasses, that's why," Dad replied. Mom tried to limit Dad's exposure to television because he yelled at it so much. He didn't do it as much with Aubrey around, but he still had his jaw clenched.

"For a lot of reasons, Aubrey, none of them good," Mom said. "There are people out there who hate folks for being a different color than they are, and they'll do terrible things to keep them beneath them, even though they're the ones who are low. Hating like that is wrong."

Dad looked up. "What are you telling him that for? It's not always wrong to hate." He pointed at the smoldering ruin on TV and said, "We've got a duty to hate people who do that."

"They think so, too," Mom muttered.

"It's different. Those people hate blacks for what they are. We hate people for what they do. This isn't some difference of opinion at a book club meeting or something. Those assholes bombed a church. They killed little girls, for Christ's sake."

"Ted," said Mom, looking pointedly at Aubrey and I to signal he might be going a little far.

"I didn't spend two years risking my ass stopping the Nazis to have them sprout up again in my country," Dad mumbled to his peas.

My father didn't talk much about the war. Some fathers do, bragging about it all the time to their sons, talking about how they felt alive and valuable when they were over in Europe or the Pacific. Jaime's father back in Queens told all kinds of stories, exciting ones about rushing through the jungle and lobbing grenades into bunkers.

Not my dad. He hadn't kept any of his Navy stuff, and all he ever said about what he'd seen and done was, "I blew things up and got out alive, okay? Let's drop it."

He sat staring at the television. Then he looked away.

"Turn that off, will you?" he said. "Christ."

II

By October, all the leaves in Innsmouth had fallen and the gray trees left behind stood scratching toward the sky. It was beautiful, more so than Flushing had been in the autumn, and our neighbors started burning the firewood they'd been laying in for the rest of the year.

It was clear by then that we'd learned all we could from the people in town, and the only place with any answers was the Maracaibo Explorer. How we'd get to it was the subject of some debate between me and Aubrey until I struck upon the idea of sneaking away from a campout.

There are mixed opinions about camping in the fall, but I'm for it. When else is it worth having a campfire if it's not getting chilly at night? That was always the symbol of camping for me, not so much the musty old tents or the soot-patchy cooking pots but a fire going in the middle of everything with everyone gazing in. The trouble with most Scouts is they're pyromaniacs at heart, throwing in cans and candy wrappers and old bottles to see them die, but I didn't think Aubrey would have that problem.

The problem Aubrey and I did have, though, was finding a way to camp without adult supervision. If our plan to sneak out to the rig was ever going to work, we'd need a good three hours when our parents didn't care what we were doing. That meant the middle of the night, and it meant being out of their sight.

Aubrey, of course, had a brilliant plan for this.

"It's easy. We camp out in the back garden of my house. The colonel has his last brandy in the den by seven o'clock, and Mother is nervous about strangers. They'll never bother us."

Getting their permission wasn't difficult – they indulged almost everything Aubrey wanted, and this was no exception – but I worried my parents would be more difficult.

My father wasn't. He rarely come home before midnight anymore, and then he'd eat leftovers straight over the kitchen sink. When I saw him at all, he was either sleeping in his chair or wishing he was, and our conversations didn't have a lot to them. You doing okay? Good enough.

Mom had a lot more questions, most of them around whether Aubrey would live to the end of the night sleeping in the cold. She thought we'd nearly killed him with our hike, and an overnight in a drafty tent might well finish the job.

He did most of the lawyering in his own defense.

"Mrs. Castillo, that was an isolated incident over two months ago. I've been getting stronger and learning a lot, and even if something were to go wrong, we'd be just feet from the back door to my house."

I remember Mom eyed us with a slight doubt. "What's the rush?"

I said, "What rush?"

"Why now? Why not wait until the spring and go camping for real when all of us can go?"

"There's no rush," I said. "It's just something fun to do—"

Aubrey stepped in. "The rush, Mrs. Castillo, is that to get my First Class rank and catch up to Bud, I've got to complete a camping trip. It's only going to get colder after this, and it's a long wait until April or even May. Six months is eight percent of my life."

He was an ace with lots of things, but not math.

Mom thought it over, and years later she told me she was still suspicious as hell about the whole enterprise. She figured we might smoke some cigarettes or go wandering around town, though, not take to the sea.

"Anybody shivers once, coughs once, sniffles once, you're inside that house."

"Of course," Aubrey assured her.

"You got to go to the bathroom, you do it inside. Nobody's pissing in Mrs. Marsh's garden."

Neither of us had even thought of that, but we both nodded.

She shook her head, but still said yes.

The plan we came up with was simple enough. Go through the motions of camping in Aubrey's backyard with pitching the tent and tending a fire and cooking a meal, wait until ten o'clock, and then borrow one of the boats moored at the rickety docks. We could row out the mile to the rig, do a quick circle to hear what we could hear and see what we could see, and then we'd row back.

It's the kind of plan you have when you're thirteen years old and think a mile is about as far as it takes to run around a block and the Atlantic Ocean will be smooth as the Central Park reservoir. Aubrey wasn't clear on who would do the rowing, but I figured it would be me. Which was fine because he wasn't looking so strong those days with the cuffs of his shirts and trousers swinging like bells against his body.

The night of the campout, Mom dropped me off at Aubrey's house and helped us unload the old Army surplus tent and camping gear we'd accumulated over the years. She kissed me on the top of the head and then did the same to Aubrey, but she watched us as we dragged all that stuff to the side of the mansion.

I imagined the inside would be something like Miss Havisham's house in the old *Great Expectations* movie, all dusty and British. His parents would be sitting in tall-backed velvet chairs, sipping tea, reading their ancient books with monocles. Perhaps they'd jingle a crystal bell to summon a butler with afternoon sandwiches, too, though Aubrey had never mentioned one.

I didn't get to see any of that, though. Aubrey led me around the side of the house through a tunnel of bare brambles. Our feet sank up to our ankles in fallen leaves, and it was like wading through the surf. A high stone wall surrounded the backyard, accessible by a towering iron gate.

It was funny to see tiny Aubrey rattling the latch and swinging that thing open—it was three times his size, but it made no noise or resistance.

"Oiled it," he said, as though expecting my question. "Can't have it squeaking when we sneak out tonight." As always, he'd thought of everything.

We closed the gate behind us and stood for a moment taking in the world behind the wall. If spiders cast vines instead of silk, their webs would look like Aubrey's garden. Strands of foliage wound and crawled across the marble walkways and statuary of the Marsh backyard, making it hard to tell what was alive and what was not. Orange half-moon mushrooms sprouted through cracks in the stone. One thin tree turned out to be a lamp post, and a bench turned out to be a knot of bushes. Their backyard was how the world would look if man disappeared and plants re-conquered all the things we've made.

I followed Aubrey to one corner where I dropped the tent bag laid on a clear patch of grass.

He slipped his pack off his back and leaned it against the stone wall. While I did the same, he untied the end of the tent bag and slid out the contents.

Like all camping equipment, it released a throat-itching scent of mildew when we unrolled it, the smell of countless nights in the rain and the snow and God knew what all. Aubrey laid out a ground cover tarp and slid the flattened tent above it. Then, we staked the corners and put together the wooden poles. They squeaked together at the loose joints, assembled and dis-assembled a thousand times before either of us was even born.

If we'd had more than two guys, some of the patrol would have gone out after some firewood while we secured the shelter. As it was, Aubrey and I had to gather some fallen limbs our-selves, though it wasn't until I had an armful that I realized I hadn't seen a fire pit or a grill. I doubted any parent of Aubrey's would be the type to flip burgers in a Kiss-the-Cook apron.

"Where's the fire circle?"

Aubrey waved me over to a fountain in the middle of the gar-den, long since dry and mold-stained. At its center stood a nude woman, hands held to heaven, a helmet atop her head, breasts right above our eyes. He hefted some split logs inside it, forming the classic teepee structure.

"We're building a fire in a fountain?"

"It's at waist height, easier for cooking. Plus it keeps the fire from spreading."

"Won't your folks be mad?"

"The Colonel suggested it," he said. "We never come out here, now that Mother's sick."

There was still an hour before sunset, but it's never too early for a Scout to light a fire. Aubrey lit a handful of leaves and tinder with a match, blew it into a flame, and slid it under some sticks. The fire ducked and bobbed around the wood, looking for an easy way to the sky, until it decided to burn its way through. Smoke seeped upward, sap popped, and soon a tiny flame took hold.

Aubrey went inside for our ground beef while I fashioned a grill from the greenest sticks I could find. He returned with a silver tray stacked with perfect burgers and foil-wrapped cobs of corn, something I'd never seen on a campout before.

We cooked our burgers beneath the smooth calves of the lady in the fountain. Soot blackened her body in long tiger-stripe streaks, and by the time we'd cooked and eaten our food, she looked like a woman gone native. It was the best meal I've ever eaten outside, where you're gnawing on burnt knots of flesh like a caveman.

Camping, like most of the stuff in the Scout handbook, seems better on paper than in the real world. With Jaime and Frank and the troop back in New York, we'd stay overnight in the Adirondacks and spend most of our time whittling and tying and digging things to be half as comfortable as we were at home. Nobody was ever as clean and happy as the boys in the handbook, and they sure didn't do any of the cool things they were supposed to do like explore the area with compasses or identify the constellations. The good thing about Aubrey was that for all he knew, that's the way things were.

We leaned back in the Marshes' garden chairs, waiting for the sun to set. The light dimmed, and the yellows and oranges of the fallen leaves turned to gray. A slight breeze hinted it would be a chilly night. You could see the stars coming out one by one, and I figured it would be any minute before Aubrey started pointing out constellations I'd never heard of.

Instead, he brought up something I didn't expect.

"What was your old Scout troop like?"

"Not as good as this one," I said.

"You never talk about your old friends or any of the things you did."

"Well," I said slowly, "that's because...it's because they were assholes and I became an asshole, too. Maybe a worse one."

I didn't swear too much around Aubrey, but there was no other word for those guys. Or for me.

"How were you an asshole?" He pronounced it carefully, like someone sipping a new drink.

"It's really, you know..."

We sat for a moment under the statue, and she seemed for me to be waiting to spill as much as Aubrey was.

"So my old troop back in Flushing met in the basement of the Lutheran church, and the Senior Patrol Leader — the boy in charge of the whole troop — was this guy named Jaime. We'd been buddies for years, but he was getting older, ogling girls all the time and saying nasty things to them across the street. You know the type."

Aubrey didn't, but he said nothing.

"The meeting was supposed to start at six on the dot, and when I was Senior Patrol Leader, it did. But on this night, a bunch of guys were hanging around the lectern at the front of the room, grunting their laughter like apes, looking at something in Jaime's hand."

Aubrey nodded.

"So I walk up to them holding out my wrist watch, and I'm about to say, 'Are we getting this show on the road or what?', but then I see what they're looking at. Jaime's got a *Playboy* centerfold opened, and his buddies are all making crude comments about what they'd do to the woman."

"What's a centerfold?"

"It's a part of a magazine that opens out to a big picture of a naked woman."

"Why would—"

I held up my hand. "It's not important. What I said was they better not have it in a Scout meeting, much less a church, and Jaime comes stepping up to me to say, 'Don't you like girls?' Which wasn't the point."

"What was the point?"

I'd been wondering that myself ever since then, and I still hadn't figured out the single reason why I'd gotten so angry about them looking at a picture.

"I don't know. Part of it was that Jaime had been elected Senior Patrol Leader instead of me, and here he was being a jackass. Another part was that, yeah, we were in a church. But the last part...well, I've been reading this book of my mom's, and I couldn't stop myself from thinking of what those guys would do that woman if she were right there in front of them and nobody was looking. It wouldn't be nice, and if it went on too long, it wouldn't be safe."

"So what did you do?"

"It wasn't exactly a fight. I mean, I swung my fist and got Jaime right in the jaw, but it was mostly me flailing my arms at all the boys coming to grab me. I was kicking behind me, shoving some kid away, and at one moment, I had someone's arm in my grasp. I'm not sure if I lost my footing or what, but something made me twist the arm until I felt the shudder of it rolling from the socket."

Aubrey's eyes were wide.

"It ended quick. The boy with the arm was Jaime and he was screaming like I'd torn it out. I thought I had, but then I saw how it was hanging down the left side, much closer to the back than it should be."

"Ah, a dislocation," Aubrey said. "Simple."

"If I'd been rational, I'd have stayed to help. But instead I just ran off into the night like a werewolf or something. When I made it home, I was somehow afraid to go inside, so I ran back to the church to see if there was an ambulance. There wasn't, so I ran back home again."

"That's it?"

"That's it?" I said. "I almost tore a boy's arm out of his socket, just because I was mad."

"No, you didn't. You couldn't have. He helped you, maybe

by falling back or being shoved in the fight, but you couldn't just have done it with your own strength."

"Well, it doesn't matter. I started the situation and I got out of control, just like my dad does. It's like a curse."

Aubrey considered this for a few moments.

"When this happens to your dad, what does he do?"

"One time when a car cut us off in traffic, we chased it down until the guy pulled into the parking lot of a church. He was the groom, and we drove off."

"No, I mean afterward."

"He doesn't do anything afterward. It just kind of...passes."

"See?" Aubrey said. "There's what's different: you think about it and regret it. That's the next step forward you're taking that he can't, like Dr. Brunner's evolution. You're learning to control it, like a superpower."

"Being pissed off isn't a superpower, Aubrey," I said.

"Depends on what you use it for," he said.

"Then what's your power?"

Aubrey said, "I don't have one."

"Oh, come on. You're good at lots of things. You're good at studying, for one. You're good at figuring things out. You can calculate things in your head. You're—" I struggled for the word a moment. "—enthusiastic, right? You do things harder than most people. You're determined. You'll go a long way when you grow up."

Aubrey considered. "Sometimes I don't know if I'm going to grow up at all."

For a kid younger than me, he sure thought a lot more about death.

"I'm not sure I can imagine it," he said. "Being bigger. Going to work. I wonder if growing up's for people who can see themselves grown up. I just see myself being me."

Looking at him there, sitting in the flickering shadows, I realized I couldn't imagine him grown up, either. I couldn't imagine him any bigger than he was. I couldn't see his wife or his children. I couldn't see him behind the wheel of a car. He seemed as frozen in time as all those pictures in the handbook, blessed or doomed to build signal towers in the woods forever.

Or maybe I hoped so.

A sliver of light widened into the courtyard and a long shadow in a dress grew across it in our direction. We turned, and standing in the doorway was a woman wearing white from her veil to her feet. I tried not to notice the outline of her body visible in silhouette through the material, though I remember it was thin with heavy knots at the elbows and knees.

"Boys?" The voice coming from the woman had a heavy accent, and it sounded like "boice."

"Mother, this is Bud Castillo. Bud, this is my mother."

I stood from beside our campfire and started to lean forward for a handshake, but Aubrey's mother leaned subtly the other way and I took the hint. She glided—there was no other word for how she moved—toward us with a tray of cookies in her hands.

"Poor Psyche," she said, looking up at the statue. "At least she's warm." Then, turning to me, she said, "I'm so pleased to meet you."

"I'm pleased to meet you too," I said.

This close to her, I could see her breath moving the lower

half of the veil in and out. Sometimes, when the flickering light caught it right, I thought I could see the unclosing mouth underneath, wide and thin-lipped. You'd think that would freak me out, but somehow it didn't. Somehow it seemed like something different and interesting about her, part of who she was.

"We're glad Aubrey found you," she said. She reached out for my shoulder. I could see for a fraction of an instant the skin on her arm was patchy with peeled skin, just like Aubrey's.

My throat knotted. That was the nicest thing anyone had ever said to me.

"I'm glad he did, too," I croaked.

She set the tray of cookies – lemon moons, I remember – on a low stone wall.

"You are good boice," she said in her accent. "Don't stare too long at Psyche."

"No, ma'am," I said.

She stepped tenderly to the door, opened it, and disappeared into the darkness inside.

Aubrey shook his head. "She's weird."

"I wonder where she gets it," I said.

We didn't speak much after that, staring at the fire and eating our lemon cookies. The lights of the Marsh house, like the others in the neighborhood, went out one by one. Soon, with the moon high in the sky and all the windows dark, it was time for us to go.

I2

Every Scout, no matter how strait-laced or even cowardly, has snuck out of a tent with his buddies on a brisk night; it might as well be a merit badge. I think it has to do with why you go to the woods in the first place, hoping something cool will happen to you. Sometimes you have to go out of your way to find it first.

With your eyes straining to see by the light of the stars and your ears open for the Scoutmaster, maybe you're especially sensitive to every feeling and sensation. You climb out of your sleeping bag and whisper to your friends through chattering teeth because, hey, something could happen and you're not going to miss it. I'd done it lots of times with Jaime and Frank in the Adirondacks, but seeing Aubrey there hunched beside the tent in his gray sneaking clothes with a big grin reminded me of how it was supposed to feel.

"You ready?" I asked, though I didn't have to. I knew that eagerness in the muscles and bones, almost ready to go on without me.

"Yeah," he replied. He twisted open the lid on a can of shoe polish. "Put some of this on your face to cut down the glare."

I took the tin from him and closed it again. "There's a fine line between 'hard to see' and 'suspicious,' Aubrey."

He considered a second. "You're right."

I looked up at the second-floor windows. A dim yellow light flickered between heavy curtains. "You sure they're asleep?" I whispered.

"Mother can't sleep most nights now," he said. "Her hearing, too, is getting less sensitive."

Good lord, I thought. What was wrong with her? Or with him?

"We'd better be careful," he said.

We left the walled garden along a path of mossy bricks to deaden the sound of our steps, and Aubrey's oiled gate swung open in perfect silence. He gave me a thumbs up and I returned it.

We turned down the sidewalk and headed for the harbor. The moonlight wasn't great for stealth, but we did the best we could by moving in the shadows with all the care and strategy of chess pieces. We walked quietly as instructed by the handbook, heel first and then the toe, but the swish of leaves blowing down the street more than covered any sound we made.

Back in Flushing, older folks went to bed early, but in Innsmouth, most occupied houses had at least one lit window still blazing after midnight. In some, there were the barely moving silhouettes of someone awake, maybe reading or maybe just waiting for the morning to come. The ones sitting sideways didn't bother me, but some seemed to be gazing out toward the streets. If any of them saw us, they made no sign of it.

"Lot of insomniacs in town?" I whispered to Aubrey.

He glanced up at the second story window where Dr. Brunner sat hunched over something and replied, "People around here don't need much sleep."

We made our way to the docks on the eastern shore, and if they were creepy during the day, they were terrifying at night: gray and splintered with black water clopping against the pilings. There were boats moored to some of them, but when we got closer, we could see the bottoms had rotted out and they'd sunk into the mud. When I found one that seemed seaworthy, Aubrey stopped me from climbing in.

"We've got to take one of their boats," he said, nodding toward the glinting lights of the rig out in the harbor.

"They'll hear the motor, if they don't see us first."

"They see boats like that all the time. But a rowboat coming slowly at night...it will catch their attention."

So we found where the Innsmouth Oil Speculating Consortium kept several Zodiacs. Those are the inflatable boats with the rough canvas sides that you see divers use, and these were each big enough for maybe half a dozen guys and some cargo. I stepped into one facing seaward so at least we wouldn't have to turn around, and I took my place beside the motor. We'd learned to steer these at Camp Flying Eagle, so I was confident I could do it.

Starting it, though, took more tries than I expected, yanking the cord over and over again with each pull making the engine growl a little louder and longer. It finally turned over in a puff of black greasy smoke and we were on our way. Aubrey sat in front to navigate.

He didn't do much of that, if I'm honest. He seemed a little distracted by staring into the water and letting one hand trail along the surface. It was almost like he was hypnotized, and I had to call him twice to snap him out of it when we made it to the rig.

He shook his head like someone waking up and then pointed to the side where I was already heading.

Dad had called it a "jack-up" rig, smaller than most and used in shallow water. This one was about the size of a baseball field. The deck was maybe thirty or forty feet above the water, so we both stared up as we steered between the pylons.

At the landward side was a metal grating platform with the occasional swell of seawater splashing up through it. Two other Zodiacs were tied up, and Aubrey managed to get our line around one of the open cleats with two attempts.

The reality of boarding this towering thing hit me when I saw the narrow ladder leading all those forty feet up to the deck. I wondered if Aubrey had the arms to pull himself up that many rungs, and then I wondered if even I did.

He seemed confident we could, and he stepped out of the boat and onto the little platform. I followed, though I couldn't let myself look down. See, unlike my dad, I'm nervous about the ocean, all that water going down and down forever with God knew what waiting for you to fall in. All my life, Dad had told me too much going on down there for anything to care about us, but I didn't get that feeling over Devil's Reef. It was nothing I could see, but I felt like I was trespassing in someone's living room.

"Come on," Aubrey said, climbing onto the first rung.

"Why are you going first?"

"In case you need to catch me," he said.

The confidence was touching, but if that happened, we'd be falling into the water together. Aubrey was light, but I wasn't Charles Atlas in the lifting department.

We climbed rung by rung, and the wind seemed to pick up the higher we got. It wasn't hard to hold on because I was never more scared of letting go of something in my life, and I think the same was true for Aubrey. I watched him grab each bar and pull himself up, and I followed right behind.

We could hear footsteps above us on the grating, and that gave me a moment of terror. What if they guarded the ladder? Or, even if they didn't, what if it was right in the middle of everything, where people were walking past all the time? The closer we got to the top, the more I wanted to cut and run while we still hadn't been caught.

But then, Aubrey would never know what they were doing out there, and neither would I.

He stopped with the top of his head barely above the deck, turning to check for anyone. Then he climbed over, turned around, and waved at me to hurry up. I did, but I made the mistake of glancing down as a wave washed over the little platform below, and seeing it vanish and then reappear through the foam turned my elbows weak.

"Come on!" he said again as loudly as he dared, and I scrambled up that last six feet.

On the deck of the rig, it looked like a bunch of metal-sided sheds sitting on top of a power plant. There were cables and wires all over, and some of the buildings seemed to hum with machinery inside. Toward the center of the rig there stood what I assumed was the actual drill.

We hurried between two sheds where we barely fit both at once.

"We should try to go to the bridge or whatever they call it," Aubrey said. "That's where the answers are."

"It's also where the 'getting caught' is, too."

We slid along a narrow gap to get closer to a two-story box-like structure with observation windows on all four sides of the second floor. Lights shone from it in all directions, and inside I could see dials and gauges and switches along the walls. I could also see Reverend Pritchett, who was peering through the window trying his best to see the surface of the water. He held a phone receiver in both hands like you'd imagine girls do when they're talking late at night about boys, kind of sneaky and intimate at the same time.

"Who's he talking to?" I asked, not particularly to Aubrey.

"Not too hard to find out," he said, pointing to a cable leading from the tower along the deck. We followed it to the edge where it dangled into the ocean and out of sight.

"Maybe your dad?" Aubrey suggested.

"Can't be," I said. "Dad's helmet doesn't have a hook up for that."

We stared down at the wire as it creaked against the metal decking with the current until the door to the control room slammed shut behind us. We ducked out of sight just in time for Pritchett to come running by, shouting to men about thirty yards away.

"He's not done! He can't be done!"

I watched as the men reeled my father's air hose up and then helped him climb off a ladder. He dropped to his knees and tapped the side of the helmet, and Mr. Pym rushed forward to unlatch it. When they got it off, my dad knelt gasping for a moment, waving people away.

Pritchett arrived then, not wearing his cheerful mask.

"I'm beginning to doubt your commitment to the project, Mr. Castillo," he said.

Dad looked up at him with one eye squinted, and I thought this was it: he'd tell Reverend Pritchett to pound sand or shove it where the sun don't shine or, if he wasn't feeling creative, simply to fuck himself. And then we'd be on our way back to New York tomorrow.

Which would have been fine by me, if we could take Aubrey with us. Maybe we'd find him a doctor in Queens better than Brunner.

I guess Dad didn't have the wind in his lungs to yell back at Pritchett. He pointed instead back where he'd come and said with a calmness that was scarier, "I can only do thirty minutes at a time. It's a mess down there still. Someone blew it to hell."

"Yes, yes," Pritchett said. "Your Navy used it as a target range."

Dad shook his head. "Not at all those angles."

Aubrey tapped my shoulder as they continued to argue. When I turned, he said, "Look. He didn't hang up the phone."

On a panel in the control room, the receiver slowly turned back and forth from its cord.

"Want to find out who it is?"

The conversation my father was having seemed far more interesting for our mission, but before I could say so, Aubrey was hurrying toward the shack. It would have been a terrible idea to split up, so all I could do was follow. Again, as I often did with him.

He clambered up the steps, hunched low so nobody could see us through the windows. The room was bright, so anything above a crouch would give us away.

We both stared at the phone a moment, and I could hear a voice faintly coming from the speaker.

I glanced at Aubrey and he glanced at me, and he took the receiver and held it up to his ear.

"Hello?" he said, deepening his voice but not in a convincing way. "No, it isn't. Who is this?"

He strained to listen, holding his other hand over his ear. Then his face took on an expression of total fear and panic. He bolted from the room, not seeming to care much if he was seen.

I was about to follow, I meant to follow, but I just had to hear for myself what it was.

Who it was.

I picked up the phone, lifted it to my ear, and heard a voice rasping the same thing over and over: *"Aubrey, when are you coming home, Aubrey?"*

"Who the hell is this?" I yelled, but then the voice stopped.

I heard the door swing open and looked up expecting that Aubrey was back. Instead it was Constable Connaghan, and he had his revolver aimed at me. I laughed.

"Are you going to shoot me?" I asked.

"If I have to," he said, stepping aside for Pritchett and several of the other men to drag me out.

13

That was the first time getting dragged out from somewhere by a cop, but it wasn't my last. Connaghan steered me toward the ladder by the collar of my jacket, and I was relieved to see Mr. Pym pulling Aubrey in the same direction.

Aubrey seemed more spooked than I'd ever seen him, squirming in Mr. Pym's grasp like a desperate fish, and Brunner stepped in to take one of Aubrey's arms much more roughly than I thought he had to. My father was watching us all with the skin between his eyes bunched like it did when he got angry, but his glances at Pritchett made me wonder just who he was angry with.

Pritchett seemed almost glad to see us.

"Visitors!" he said, arms open wide. "I'm surprised it took so long, a couple of curious boys like you. Did you find what you wanted to see? Hear what you wanted to hear?"

Neither of us had the guts to reply, but Pritchett nodded like he'd expected so.

"Well, it's getting colder and wetter out here, and we can't have either one of you taking sick. Let's all go back to shore together and discuss this like men." He motioned to Brunner, whispered something in his ear, and then sent him away to the command shack.

It was Brunner. He'd seen us after all and called Connaghan. Truly the act of a highly evolved being, perhaps a rat.

Pritchett descended the ladder first, and Connaghan nudged me to go next. By then, it had gotten even colder and the wind blasted between us and those rungs so it was hard to hang on. Aubrey came after me, staring toward the water with horror.

"Are you okay?" I asked him, and he shook his head.

My dad came last, and when all four of us were on the lower deck, Pritchett swept his hand toward one of the Zodiacs for us all to board. My father sat by the engine and steered us back to shore without saying a word or changing his expression. Pritchett wasn't saying much either, just smiling like a man about to go fishing.

Aubrey was shivering and rocking back and forth, which I assumed were signs he was getting sick again like he had after the hike. I was halfway taking off my jacket to give him when I heard the splash of him diving into the harbor.

"Aubrey!" I shouted, rushing to the side and reaching for him. All I could see was his feet sliding away beneath the surface. "Stop the boat! He's gone over!"

Dad slowed the engine and made to turn, but Pritchett shook his head.

"Bullshit," my father muttered. "Kid can barely survive on land."

Another Zodiac departed the rig behind us and began sweeping a searchlight across the harbor.

"They have it in hand," Pritchett said. "We're not equipped for a rescue."

It was true. We had a single small lantern and no rope I could see except for the short line for tying up to a dock. Still, we had to help. I climbed toward the front of the boat, and Pritchett shoved me back into my seat.

"I said they have it in hand," he said. "I guarantee he's safer than you."

We sat in the idling boat a moment, my father looking Pritchett over as though deciding whether we should throw him overboard next. I was ready to help, sure I could get under his feet so Dad could finish the job with a quick punch to the jaw, but to my surprise, Dad revved the motor instead and sped us back to the crumbled docks of Innsmouth. I watched behind us for any sign of Aubrey, but the men on the rig were already sweeping their lights across the water.

The drive to our house was silent and awkward, and when we arrived, the lights shone from our windows.

Pritchett entered our own house before we did, opening the door like he knew it was unlocked and stamping his feet on the welcome mat. He stepped inside, looked around, and said, "I see everything's in hand here, too."

"Ginnie!" my father yelled.

Pritchett took on a regretful expression. "Mrs. Castillo is visiting with some friends for the time being."

"Where? What friends?"

"She's fine. If anything, she's better than she's been in weeks, not having to take care of the two of you." He checked his watch. "She's in her guest bed by now after a chamomile tea and some womanly conversation."

Dad lunged forward and lifted Pritchett by the front of his

coat. The reverend, smiling, let himself hang in my father's grasp until he set him down.

"Mr. Castillo, I understand your distress and confusion. A lot has happened, and I think we're good enough neighbors now to discuss it in the open."

"Neighbors," my father said.

"And you could be family. That's all we've ever wanted in Innsmouth, to be a family again. We're so close, and I can see it was a mistake to leave you in the dark so long."

"About what?"

"Young master Castillo here knows," he said. "Don't you?"

"There's someone down there under the reef."

Pritchett nodded. "Got it in one. How did you realize it?"

"I talked to him on the phone."

My dad shook his head. "What phone?"

"You haven't been on the northeast zone for a few weeks, but we dangled a wire for some friends," Pritchett said.

"Friends? What are they breathing?"

"Sea water. Through slits in their necks, if I'm told correctly."

Dad spoke slowly now, a little like someone talking a suicidal person off a ledge.

"That's what we're drilling for? To get some imaginary people out?"

Pritchett laughed. "No, Mr. Castillo. We're drilling to get us *in*. All of us, the people of Innsmouth, the kin of those who were killed and imprisoned four decades ago. Our birthright of life eternal was taken from us, and thanks to you, we're within reach of it once again. The getting out will come later when our numbers grow."

Dad shook his head. "You know, it's almost a relief."

The reverend blinked in surprise.

"Sincerely. I gotta tell you the odds of oil down there are nil, and I've been feeling this whole time like I was stealing your money. But if there are people down there like you say, then I'm all for getting them out."

Pritchett narrowed his eyes. "You believe me?"

"Mister, I couldn't count for you all the things in this world I don't believe in. And you know how much my lack of belief matters? Not a bit. Things either are or they aren't, and blowing a hole in a reef is pretty much the same whether there's oil inside or people."

"It doesn't matter to you?" Pritchett asked, which was the same question I had.

"What matters to me is this kid" — my father jabbed a thumb in my direction — "and my wife. So if you could bring her home, I'm just as happy getting back to work."

Pritchett shook his head. "I'm sorry to say, Mr. Castillo, that won't be possible. In these critical days, we're going to need your full attention — and your son's — on finishing our project. Mrs. Castillo will be living in far greater comfort than she has been, and when we make it through and you see her again, you'll find she's gained some comfortable weight from all the cookies and finger sandwiches she's been eating."

There was a clue: she might be with the Spivey sisters who were known for their genteel gatherings. But then, who knew if the Spivey sisters were in their home or somewhere else.

"Well, we might be at an impasse, then," Dad said. "Explosives are dangerous, and I may not be able to focus as—"

"Mrs. Castillo's continued comfort relies upon that focus, Mr. Castillo."

That stopped Dad short.

"Can I talk to her?"

"I'm sure a nightly call can be arranged for the duration of the project. How long do you think it might be?"

"Three weeks at most," Dad said.

"Ah, barely a vacation." Pritchett rose. "I had a feeling we could come to an understanding."

He put on his hat but paused at the door.

"We're not monsters, you know."

"We can tell," I said.

"Monsters hurt other people. They put them in hospitals and do experiments on them and blow up their homes. They spray them with firehoses and bomb their churches. They put their mamas in jail just for praying to better gods. What we want is to go to a place where there are no missiles, no racists, no armies, no deaths. With the blessings of our friends, we will swim forever free from the burdens of human weakness."

He opened the door.

"And when the time comes, you will beg to join us."

14

The days following sucked, not to put too fine a point on it. I became my father's apprentice, and he was less happy about it than I was.

"Don't get to liking this," he told me. "You're still going to college to be a lawyer or something."

There wasn't much fear of me liking it. We were up around four each morning for a quick breakfast standing in our empty kitchen, and then we'd drive down to the docks where a sullen jump-suited employee of the Innsmouth Oil Speculating Consortium was waiting for us to board a Zodiac. He often took off before we were even seated, and we'd both fall back onto the plank seats as the boat slapped across the breakers toward the rig.

Once we climbed the swaying ladder to the deck, our workday began. That entailed setting up Dad's equipment for him and helping him into his suit, tightening the bolts on the brass helmet and checking the hose connections. I ran the compressor while he descended below the surface with satchels of Primacord hanging from his belt.

Then I waited with Dad's supervisor, Mr. Charrier. He'd lean against the wall away from the wind and spray, smoking cigars one after the other while I hunkered shivering by the compressor. There was no shelter for me, just the makeshift tent of an oversized rain slicker I'd pull over my head.

Sometimes the compressor would conk out, which was terrifying. Often it was as simple as restarting the motor, but other times I'd have to spray a solvent on the moving parts because they were coated with salt. I'd have to adjust the choke, pull the starter, and hope it got going again.

Meanwhile, Dad would be down there gasping for air while fighting the movement of the water like a man walking in a hurricane.

"It's a mess on the bottom," he told me. "Wreckage from ships, torpedo casings, and rubble everywhere. All I've got is the helmet light, so an old cable or a boulder could be a foot away until I see it."

On days with actual explosions when they triggered the Primacord, Dad would come back up to the deck and they'd give me the honor of flipping the switches, not a big plunger like in the cartoons. When I did it, a huge cloud of bubbles would roil to the surface, and there'd be a roar like each of them was holding the sound of the explosion.

I'd help Dad remove the suit, and then I'd give him some coffee from the Thermos. Charrier would graciously allow us into the shack and out of the wind so Dad wouldn't freeze to death, but he was also the one who tapped on his watch to remind us it was time to go back down.

We'd do that four or five times a day, and my father would look worse after each one — gray-skinned and sunken-eyed. Charrier usually insisted on one more dive than I wanted.

Sometimes Pritchett would come to talk to me while my father was under the rig, and he kept trying to sell it to me like my opinion mattered to him.

"These aren't bad people, Bud. I'm not a bad person," he told me on one of those occasions.

"Okay," I said, keeping an eye on the compressor.

"As you grow up, I think you'll find nobody's bad. They just have different purposes than yours, a different way of thinking. How many ants do we kill in a year? To them, we're the apocalypse."

"Everybody in town okay with your apocalypse?"

"They are now," he said. "I've been out to the hospital just like you have, and I've brought them back the files of their loved ones. They know everything that happened, everything the people from Away did to them, and they're fine as rain with whatever it takes to get them back."

"It was you there that day."

He nodded. "I had a suspicion young master Aubrey would take an outsider there. I had no objection because we'd have to tell you sooner or later."

"What happened?"

His expression darkened. "Better people than their captors had enough, that's what happened. They fought back and won, and the ones who could went to their true homes."

"Where did they go?"

He pointed through the deck.

If my dad was a betting man, he'd have placed odds at millions to one that there were people living in the reef. I'd heard the voice on the phone, so I'd put it at maybe three to one. Still, there was still the real possibility that every person in Innsmouth was crazy as a shithouse rat, as my dad liked to say.

"And they just...live there? Stuck?"

"The Deep Ones rule a kingdom beneath the reef of unimaginable grandeur and majesty."

"Deep Ones? That's what they're called?"

"Not by themselves, but it's close enough for us."

"And you're not a Deep One, right? You'd have turned into one by now."

Pritchett seemed to get defensive at that. "Not all people transform at the same time of their lives. For some it comes late."

"Or not at all, right, like for some of the folks in town," I said. "Got it. What makes you think they're going to let you in?"

He leaned back from me in surprise. "My mama was their loyal servant in the swamps of Louisiana for many years. She knew some of their magic and spread their ways, at least until people like you put her away in a house of stone. The Deep Ones show their gratitude in wondrous ways."

"You're doing all this because you think they'll pay you back?"

With no answer, he walked away.

When we'd done what they considered a day's work, we were taken back to the shore via the Zodiac again in the dark. I'd watch the few working lights of Innsmouth glinting in the distance, thinking Aubrey was right: they'd be almost impossible to see if you had to swim, and I wondered every time if he'd made it to shore.

Nobody would tell me no matter how many times I asked. Pritchett would only say Aubrey was "safe from you, at least."

Which I guess wasn't wrong.

We'd drive home in the Volkswagen, sometimes with Constable Connaghan following in the Nash police cruiser. When Connaghan was busy elsewhere, we'd take a spin up and down a few streets in case we could see some sign of where Mom was being kept. I guess we figured she'd hang a handkerchief outside a window at least, but we never saw one.

We'd arrive at the house, eat our canned dinner standing in the kitchen, and then take turns in the shower. Sometimes they'd let Mom call, and we'd each have a few minutes of conversation with her.

"Everything okay?" was Dad's usual question, and her usual answer was that it was, though painfully boring. He'd tell her we were working as fast as we could.

The first time I got to speak to her, I told her I was sorry for sneaking away from the campout and getting us all into trouble.

"It's okay, Buddy," she said. "I think we were already in trouble."

So went our days and then our weeks.

"We could be doing something, you know," I said one night on the way home with the heater groaning.

Dad held the wheel with both hands, though there was nothing in the road.

"We are doing something," he said. "We're doing what smart people always do, which is humor the strong stupid ones until they're bored with us and move on."

"No, I mean, we could be talking to people on the rig, or

sending a note to Aubrey somehow, or sneaking out—"

"Bud, this isn't the Hardy Boys. It's life. It's growing up. It's realizing sometimes you're lucky to avoid horrible people and sometimes you're not."

So that was it. People like Pritchett were storms to be weathered, hiding somewhere in a cellar. I knew my father was tired and I knew he thought the Scout handbook was a bunch of crap that nobody but suckers believed in, but to me, he seemed just as terrible as any bad guy. Maybe worse because he knew better.

Which is why I felt brave enough to say, though quietly, "Is that how we won the war?"

He glanced sharply at me. "Here's the secret, Buddy: we didn't win the war. We slowed down one specific group of assholes until they could slither away through the cracks to Bonn or Paris or Sao Paolo or Washington where now they wear suits. They're everywhere. They've always been everywhere, and you could drive yourself crazy hunting them down in all four corners of the world when new ones are being made daily right next door. God knows I have."

"Dad, these people aren't Nazis. They're old and confused or something. Aubrey's not a Nazi."

"I don't know what Aubrey is," he said.

If I'd been any less exhausted, I'd have either jumped out of the Volkswagen at the next stop sign or socked my dad in the jaw for saying that. Maybe there's a moment when you know you're growing up, when you consider that your father not only could be hurt by a punch from you but might actually deserve one.

What I said instead was, "Aubrey is sick, just like the people from that hospital we found in the woods. It isn't his fault and it wasn't theirs, and it's all connected to the reef you're helping Pritchett open up again."

Dad leaned back in his seat. Then he took his cigarettes from his shirt pocket, tapped one out of the pack, and lit it. "Assuming you saw what you think you saw, we're living in a town full of people from a loony bin, people who wish they could turn into monsters and are paying me a bundle to help them drill the bottom of the ocean to find more of their monster friends. Is that the shape of it?"

"I heard them."

"You heard voices at the end of a phone. God knows where that wire leads, maybe even back to the surface."

"They knew Aubrey's name."

"You heard Aubrey's name."

I turned in my seat, flushed. "Are you trying not to believe me?"

He let the cigarette droop from the side of his mouth as he turned the key to restart the Volkswagen. "I'm trying to think of a way we can get out of these people's way before they kill themselves and us with them."

"How can you believe Vietnam is an excuse to sell bullets and planes but you won't believe me?" There went the Scout Law in one sentence. There went loyalty, obedience, and most of the others. "Dive down there, try the telephone yourself. Go to the hospital in the woods."

What was wrong with him? Why wasn't Castillo Syndrome kicking in, making him want to fight? What was the point of being reckless and dumb half the time if he wouldn't be reckless and dumb when it helped for a change?

"So you're not going to stop them?" I asked.

"Bud, look at me. I blow things up for a living. You know why I do that instead of working in a cushy office on Fifth Avenue? Because all my life, I've taken a lot of bone-headed chances trying to 'do good,' and they've only gotten me into trouble. My new plan? Live well, keep out of trouble, and pick my battles. The Scout Law's all good for kids like you, but the big rule you follow as an adult is that you don't shit where you sleep."

He turned into our driveway. The engine rattled to a stop.

"Do I want to stay here with a bunch of screwballs?" he said. "Of course not. But a life of fighting has gotten me where I am today, stuck working for them. We're going to help dig their little fort underground and then we're getting the hell out of here. That's what we're doing."

I didn't reply or make any move to get out of the bus.

He let go of the wheel and turned to me. "There are a couple hundred of them and three of us, and I'm too old to be crashing myself against the whole stinking human race to save them. Every time I do it, it kills me a little more. Worse, it kills your mother a little more. People aren't going to clap you on the back for 'saving' them like they do in the Scout handbook. They're going to hate you. They may even hurt you."

I gazed through the windshield at our house, still not getting out.

"But you're not buying it, are you?" he asked.

"No, I get it. I understand."

Dad opened his door. "If you really did, you'd sock me in the jaw."

15

The outside world of Away may not have been welcome in Innsmouth, but they couldn't stop radio waves. While I was chattering my teeth nearly to dust on that dangerous rusty hulk of an oil rig, I could sometimes get away with playing WRKO out of Boston on my portable Magnavox. A lot depended on the mood of my dad's boss Mr. Charrier, but I think even he got some kicks out of DJ Arnie Ginsburg. God knew we needed some kicks.

There's not much in this world more surreal than hearing "Surfin' U.S.A." or "Heat Wave" under a dull-gray dome of clouds while black waves splash against the pylons, except maybe Mr. Pym in a yellow rain slicker plodding in time with "Walk Like a Man." When he and some of the other guys would pause to listen, it gave me my first inkling that Pritchett didn't have all their hearts and souls.

Around 1:40 on the twenty-second of November, some dumb song like "If I Had a Hammer" dropped away with a squeak of feedback and was replaced by a breathless reporting saying, "News from Dallas: there has been a gun attack on the President of the United States."

By chance, Dad happened to be between dives and he frowned first at me and then at the radio. I turned it up.

"We have reports that today at 12:30 Central Standard Time, President Kennedy and Governor Connally were shot as their motorcade left the downtown area of the city."

A few of the other men began to gather around, Mr. Pym and Mr. Geiss and Mr. Olmstead, and someone turned over a bucket so my father could catch a seat in his heavy suit.

"We have no official word on the President's condition, repeat no official word, though blood was visible on the President's head as Mrs. Kennedy tried to hold her husband."

I'm not sure who gasped, maybe me.

"Governor Connally had visible chest wounds as the motorcade sped to Parkland Hospital in downtown Dallas."

Dad stared down at the deck, listening intently but shaking his head. Reverend Pritchett saw us huddled around the radio, and he arrived just in time to hear the reporter intone, "There is no reason to believe the President is dead."

In a moment of humanity I wouldn't have expected from him, Pritchett squatted beside us to listen, too. It wouldn't last long, but it was something.

"If that's a head wound, it's all over," Dad said.

Someone shushed him, again maybe me. I felt like someone floating above, watching a horrible show from fifty feet up.

Pritchett was leaning in with one ear, and I swear there was the curl of a smile at the corner of his lips.

"We're hearing now that the President arrived at Parkland face down on the floor of his limousine, which was driven today without its protective bubble top. The White House is telling reporters they have nothing beyond what we know now."

When other people talk about the Kennedy assassination, they remember it from a comfortable living room or inside a car or maybe on a street outside a TV store. For them, it went fast. For us, hunkered around the tiny radio, it seemed to go slow: five minutes, ten minutes, fifteen minutes of the same talk in circles, and then something horribly new.

"We have word now that a priest has been summoned to Parkland Hospital."

My father stood up, walked to the edge of the deck, and yelled, "Fuck!" out toward the sea. I'd have done the same if he weren't there.

It wasn't much later when the reporter said, "We have word now, official, that President John F. Kennedy was pronounced dead at 1 p.m. Central Standard Time. Lyndon Johnson, the Vice President, will presumably..."

I didn't hear much next. We all stood up and wandered around the radio, each in our thoughts. Nobody cried, but I could see fear on some of those weathered gray faces. Not on Pritchett's, though.

He rested his hand on my shoulder and said, "To the farthest perspective, all things tend toward justice."

"How you figure?" I demanded. What was he going to do to me, take away my mother and make me work with my father to blow up a reef?

"I figure it this way: your president had the good sense to have his brains shot out before he could start a war, get caught with a woman, or grow to a feeble old age. He got out, as they say, when the gettin' was good, before we all had time to realize he was a lie along with the rest of civilization."

"He's our president," I said.

"If he was anybody's president, it wasn't ours. Maybe some old white men in a paneled room somewhere smoking cigars, he could have been theirs, I don't know. What I do know is these moments of truth do all of us good. They remind us who we are, how close we still live to the jungle."

My father stood watching us, not saying anything. He seemed to be waiting to hear what I had to say next, but I wasn't in the mood for a debate.

"With all due respect, Mr. Pritchett, I don't give a flying fuck what you think of our president or about life or about this stupid goddamned reef."

The men all looked surprised by my language, though not so much my father who knew I'd inherited it honestly. Pritchett smiled.

"See? That's a start. Our freedom begins when we realize all laws but ourselves are lies."

The awful thing is he could have been right, at least a little in a deranged sort of way. Maybe my books were full of shit, bedtime stories for suckers to keep blood from running in the streets. But if my book was full of shit, so was his—and so was he.

"Oh, we're done with lying now? Aces. Where's my mother? Where's Aubrey? What's going to happen to all these people when you get through the reef?"

Pritchett didn't say anything.

I was exhausted, as though I'd been fighting him with my fists instead of my big mouth. I settled on the decking beside the radio, the voices in the speaker dying with the battery.

"I want to go home," I said, barely loud enough to hear.

Pritchett stooped beside me, almost like a coach would do.

"Your home's as dead as Kennedy, rotting somewhere on a stretcher in Dallas with his brains still in Jackie's hair."

I'm not an elegant fighter, it's true, but I'm a passionate one. All the dials inside me cranked to their max, I dove for him. My head got him right beneath the diaphragm, which I hadn't meant to do, and it sent him tumbling back on the grating and gasping for breath.

Mr. Pym and Mr. Olmstead grabbed my arms so I couldn't take another lunge, but I was out of gas for sure by then.

Pritchett leaned up on one elbow and managed to squeak, "Which Scout law was that, Bud? Courteous? Kind? Friendly?"

"It's a new one: a Scout is Pissed."

Mr. Charrier let us go home early, and once we returned to shore and got in the Volkswagen, my dad paused before turning the key.

"You done good, Buddy," he said.

I started to cry. It might have been Kennedy, it might have been Mom and Aubrey, it might have been that wretched little town, it might even have been Jaime and Frank: all of it seemed to come out at once, and I was a blubbering mess all the way home. I'd never cried that way before and I haven't often since, the weeping of deep sadness but also relief you're still able to feel it.

Dad seemed taken aback but he didn't try to stop my crying. He patted my leg instead.

"Do you...do you think it was the Russians?" I managed to

ask by the time we got to our house.

He shook his head. "They'd have done something else by now. It was probably just some asshole. God knows there are enough of them in the world."

Some asshole. Of the same species as one who'd get Martin Luther King and Robert Kennedy, another who'd send a bunch of teenagers to stab people in their Benedict Canyon houses, and even more who'd shoot villagers in Vietnam and blanket the jungle in napalm. Some asshole, genus and species.

I wasn't sleeping in the small hours that night when the pebbles tapped my window, so I threw aside the covers and made it to the sill in time to see a small figure flapping away into the cover of the trees. I noticed the flag on our mailbox was up, so I put on my coat but not my shoes to see what Aubrey had left me.

Inside the mailbox was a square envelope of fine linen sealed with a daub of wax. I tore it open and read the note penned in shaky calligraphy.

"I'm sorry about President Kennedy. I'm sorry about Innsmouth. I'm sorry."

Deep inside the mailbox, he'd left his Scout kerchief neatly folded.

16

I don't know how many thirteen-year-olds are trusted with spools of Primacord and sticks of TNT, but in December of 1963, I was one of them. If my father wasn't going to do anything to stop Pritchett, then I was.

The *Maracaibo Explorer* was a small rig, I've discovered in the years since. In its center was a crane now fitted with a drill poised ominously to open the reef and let all of Innsmouth's lost souls in…and others out.

What little I knew of demolitions of course came from my brief apprenticeship. Some fathers might have taught their boys the family business, but Dad tried to shelter me from his work. The most he showed me was how to operate the air compressor and follow his signals for descending and ascending, so that meant it was up to me to figure out how I'd destroy an oil rig.

One factor in my favor was the rig was a mess: steel walls with curls of peeling paint, grating whistling in the wind, cables going nowhere, and pipes dry of oil. It wouldn't be hard to hide explosives around any of that crap, if I knew where it would do some good. Was it worth destroying the drill itself, or was it better to sink the whole thing? I had no idea, and I wished Aubrey was around to help. He'd probably read some books on physics that would explain where best to destroy this beast.

But after the assassination, I didn't see him again. At my insistence, Dad would drive past the Marsh house on the way to the docks each morning even with Constable Connaghan following us in his Nash cruiser. Each time, though, I saw no signs of life except sometimes a light behind the kitchen window. I wondered if the one covered by the planks was Aubrey's or his mother's.

To keep them in or out, I had no way of knowing.

One day, I twisted Dad's arm into stopping out front so I could hurry to his mailbox. It was lightly raining, and Connaghan flashed his lights at me in annoyance. I put a small package in the box, raised the flag, and ducked back into the Volkswagen. Torn between making sure we got to work and finding what was in the mailbox, Connaghan chose to follow us.

So the odds weren't bad that Aubrey got what I left him: his Scout neckerchief and a note saying, "SCOUTS DON'T ALL LOOK THE SAME."

I had no idea for sure if he'd gotten it, but he didn't show at my house or at the rig. He was either too sick to come or too different than the boy he was.

Which left me to execute my plan by myself, a plan that involved squirreling away TNT as close to each corner of the rig as I could get it, trusting that some foggy night I'd be able to link it with Primacord. If I was lucky, no one would find it. If I was really lucky, no one would accidentally detonate it while Dad and I were still onboard.

It was a dumb and reckless plan, but those were traits I'd inherited honestly, after all. Dr. Brunner had said we're all the right tool for the right job, and maybe that's what Castillos were good for.

((⊖ ⊕ ⊖))

Pritchett and Brunner were strutting around the deck in those final days, pointing to the horizon and laughing like men about to send a man to the Moon. Neither acknowledged me much, which was fine by me. You can get more damage done when people think you're harmless and broken.

Brunner did stop once near the compressor to watch my father's hose slithering along the edge with me. His tie flapped over his shoulder in the wind.

"You know, when we open the reef, nobody has to be left behind again like they were in town all those years ago. They will welcome us all, the half breeds and the quarters and the eighths. Like you."

"Is that who's down there? Puerto Rican Jews?"

"You are an arrogant little boy full of other people's words, but I'll still tell you this: beneath us is a life of everlasting wonder and glory, and we will gift it even to you and your father and your mother. And soon after, we will gift it to the world. Then there will be no more missiles and no more borders and no more prejudice. Isn't that what you want?"

"Some people just sit in at lunch counters instead of releasing monsters from under the sea."

"I think soon you will see who are the monsters and who are not." He bent and set three of my planted charges beside me.

"You misplaced these."

ᐊ ᗡ ⊖ ⊕ ⊖ ᗡ ᐅ

Not long after, the men from the rig stopped taking us to shore. They set up a small sleeping space with cots in one of the empty storage bays, and we spent our resting hours there with the endless wash of the ocean echoing beneath us.

"They must be in a hurry because it's getting cold," I said to Dad one morning as we got dressed by the light of a lantern.

"They're in a hurry because we're getting close," he said, pulling on his boots. "Three more dives will do it."

"Then what?"

"Then they throw the switch, probably with praying or some shit, and then they'll blow it in two stages. This first one will loosen the rocks, and the second will blast the rubble down the westward side into deeper water. The drill will do the rest, if the reef isn't opened already."

"Can we stop it?"

Dad paused to think and then continued pulling on the other boot.

"You know, the funny thing about being the only diver on a project is nobody can check your work."

"What do you mean?"

"It's dark down there, and a man as worried about his loved ones as I am could well have placed those charges on, well, nearly anything. Even pylons."

My mouth hung open in astonishment.

"What? It was the Kennedy thing that got me because I'm a big dumb sucker. Also, I got a little inspiration from your tackle of the good reverend. Does a father proud to see his son beating up an asshole. That oughta be somewhere in your book."

"Why didn't you tell me?"

"Because you were doing just fine on your own, making them think you were going to blow up the rig from the top," he said. "And if anybody asked, I wanted you to say you didn't know anything else while still being a good Scout, in case that matters."

Until then, I'm not sure I'd ever been proud of my father. He'd been in a war, sure, and he'd provided for our family, but these were all the things you took for granted from fathers. Sometimes, I'd even been the opposite of proud of him, especially in those times when he seemed to go way too far with his feelings.

I realized then that sometimes, those feelings were for us.

"Why are you telling me now?"

"Because when the time comes to set off the charges, I'm going to need your help getting the good people off this tub and keeping the bad ones on it."

"How do we know which is which?"

"I think we already know, don't you?"

The usual crew complement of the rig was then maybe eight people, including us. We could get all of them aboard a Zodiac and back to shore.

"How fast will the rig go down?"

"There are two circuits now. The first blows the west side and the second blows the east. There's a delay between the sides, which might give us twenty minutes of steel buckling to lower us to the water. Then this old girl goes on a sleigh ride off the continental shelf."

"Might?"

"You got that swimming badge, right?"

17

When I reeled up the air hose from my father's final dive two days later, I wondered if I'd ever have to do it again. I hoped not, and so far, I've gotten my wish.

When Dad got to the top of the ladder, Pritchett and Farkas were waiting with champagne. They grinned and peered into my father's helmet window until he nodded and gave the thumbs up. While I helped him get the helmet off, Pritchett opened the bottle with the cork and foam shooting in an arc to the water. Farkas messily filled the fluted glasses sitting on a spool of Primacord.

"To opening the way!" Pritchett said, and everyone lifted their glasses. Me and my father looked down into ours, glanced at each other, and then each took a sip.

The other men aboard clapped, though not with a lot of energy. They'd been out there for six months of all the small explosions and test drillings that made this final opening so close to reality. They took large gulps of the champagne, and Mr. Pym even spilled some on the front of his blue jumpsuit.

"It's a new moon tonight, a time when the curtain between

the physical world and the spiritual one is especially thin. It will be perfect for our final ceremony."

"You really just have to flip the switches," Dad said.

There were three: one for the western circuit, another for the eastern, and a failsafe one you had to toggle first.

Pritchett shook his head chidingly. "An artist who does work as well as you do knows it's the more-than-necessary that differentiates us from the animals."

"If it's worth doing, it's worth overdoing," Dad said into his glass.

"Exactly!" Pritchett patted him on the back.

Dad looked up again. "I believe my wife and my paycheck are due?"

"All part of the ceremony tonight!" Pritchett said. "When we get what we want, you get what you want, and we all go home happy."

"Or you could just blow it right now," Dad said, glancing around at a plausible number of people to save that didn't yet include my mother. "Why wait for so many things to go wrong? A rock tumbles in the wrong place or a current pulls a wire, and you're going to look like a jackass."

"I'm not worried about the quality of your work, Mr. Castillo."

"Aren't your friends down there getting impatient by now?"

Pritchett glanced at him sharply. "They have lived there since the Earth was only ocean, and they'll live there until it's ocean again."

Dad held up his hands. "You're the money bags. I'm here to blow shit up."

"That's the spirit," Pritchett said, tossing his glass over the railing.

（ ◖ ⊖ ⊕ ⊖ ◗ ）

From what Pritchett had said about his "ceremony," we knew Mom would be on the rig that night when we detonated the charges, meaning one extra person to save, the most valuable of all.

"She's a strong swimmer," Dad said when we had a moment alone. His voice wasn't as strong as usual, though. "She was a lifeguard one summer at camp in the Catskills."

"Was the water fifty degrees?"

Dad didn't reply, gazing out over the railing instead.

"For the Lifesaving badge, they told us all about hypothermia. That's what gets you second," I said. "First, it's cold shock. It can kill someone right then and there, if they're old."

"We won't even touch the water. The charges are low, and the failing beams will give us plenty of time. We're going to stroll off this thing like the Rockefellers from the Queen Mary."

"With clothes, we'll have half an hour at most in the water. Your muscles start getting weak, making it hard to move your limbs."

Dad nodded. "In thirty minutes, we'll be on the shore, everybody having a good laugh at the time we tried to open a seal to the underworld."

He didn't seem to be getting what I was saying, so I kept at it. "The instructor said even after getting dry, people have to lie down so they don't stress their hearts. That can kill, too."

He turned to me quickly. "Who the hell taught this badge, a Titanic survivor?"

"I'm just telling you what I heard," I said.

"Controlled explosion, Buddy," he said. "Surf City, all the way down."

Any illusion there'd be anything controlled about that night went away near sundown when the flotilla set off from the Innsmouth docks. Three Zodiacs plus half a dozen battered motorboats came chugging toward the rig, some of them rolling badly over the breakers. Every one of them was full of people in evening clothes like they were going to a party.

"They're bringing the whole goddamned town," Dad muttered as they came closer.

Farkas had "asked" us to string bunting along the railings and set up tables with red, white, and blue tablecloths because all Mr. Pym could find were discount decorations from the Fourth of July. That gave everything a festive and patriotic look, even in the gloom.

One of the many bullhorn speakers on the rig squealed to life with a record of Sousa marches, the perfect start to the weirdest night of my life.

The townsfolk came up the ladder one by one, some of them with small suitcases that had to be raised with a rope and pulley. Suitcases. What could they bring to start a life immortal under the sea? Pajamas? Extra underwear? I "accidentally" tripped over one to get a clue what could be inside, and the rattle of glass inside made me realize it was either family china or framed photos.

Aubrey's parents arrived on the deck, his father in his blue military uniform and his mother still veiled in her white dress. The colonel shook our hands and thanked us for all we'd done.

"You're welcome," I said, weakly.

Dad watched Mrs. Marsh glide over to us with a kind of awe. She seemed surprised when she held out a hand to her, one that seemed to glisten slightly. He took it.

"Mrs. Marsh," he said.

"This is trouble," she said.

"You're telling me," he replied.

Some of the women were wearing heels because nobody had told them the deck was grating, so they staggered around laughing until the Spivey sisters kicked off theirs like the flappers they'd once been. Then the others did the same.

Mom was somewhere toward the end, and we ran to her the second she got off the ladder. All three of us hugged a long time, and I heard Mom say, "They're not drilling for oil." Dad replied something, but we were soon pulled out of the way for the last ones to arrive.

Connaghan was the final one up and he gave a nod to Pritchett.

The people of Innsmouth looked around in their small chatting groups beneath the gleaming strings of lights, pointing up at the drill derrick or off into the Atlantic. They grazed hors d'oeuvres, pigs in a blanket and shrimp cocktail and little kebabs of beef that my mother called "upstate wedding fare."

We didn't have much time to talk because everyone approached at least once to shake our hands and thank us for saving the town. Mom and Dad, though, kept communicating with the silent language of glances that most couples seem to have, and I could tell they didn't agree on what we should do next.

A tremendous shot exploded from somewhere behind us,

and we all gasped and turned toward the source of the noise. Pritchett stood in the middle of the deck with a chromed .357 revolver pointed to the sky. It got our attention.

"Welcome, friends!" Pritchett said, and a few people laughed uncomfortably. We didn't.

"A big night requires a big noise!" he said, which got him some applause. "And we'll be making a big noise in more ways than this in just a few hours."

My dad shook his watch on his wrist. Even a social occasion held at the barrel of a gun wasn't enough to keep him interested.

"But first, we have to say goodbye to some old friends."

Pritchett walked toward us, smiling, gun held loose at his side. I felt Dad tense up and so did I, and I figured we could both at least slam him to the ground before he got off a shot.

He walked past us, waggling an eyebrow like he'd made a funny joke. Then, he leaned over the railing and looked down toward the lower dock. He aimed and fired once. Some people flinched, but not me. I was listening for exactly what I heard: the whistling rush of air from the punctured side of an inflatable Zodiac.

Dad had said the military ones could take a few bullets, but these were cheap and with a few quick gleeful shots, they were all rolling sideways and crumbling under the water. He fired twice more into the wooden ones for good measure, but I doubted they would sink.

Pritchett turned back to the crowd. "They've served us well, but we won't need boats where we're going."

As he reloaded the pistol, Pritchett glanced up at the sky as though judging its readiness. Finding it unsatisfactory, he snapped the cylinder closed.

"Our stars have not yet come out for us, so please eat and drink while celebrating the courage that got us here...especially all of yours."

A minister with a gun tends to cool down a crowd, though the wind was helping plenty in the literal sense, too. Some of the men wore their overcoats and a few of the women had stoles, including Miss Delacroix with a white fox one.

I walked up to her to say hello.

"Oh, Bud!" she said. "I had a wonderful time with your mother these last two weeks."

Damn. I'd figured she would be too infirm to be Mom's "hostess" so I'd never bothered to check her house for a sign she was.

"I guess I'm glad," I said.

"I'm sorry about your special friend Aubrey," she said.

"Why?" I snapped. "What do you know?"

"Only that he's gone," she said. "Probably where Henry went."

We both peered down at the sea, though of course there was no chance either would be there.

"You're a good boy, Bud. I knew it before your mother told me. But good doesn't always mean right."

"Is that from the Book of Pritchett, Miss Delacroix?"

She laughed. "No. I'm just trying to tell you these are all lonely people who want one thing, a chance to be loved again. They were denied it first by their bodies and then by the government, and they're not going to give up. I'm not going to give up."

"Pritchett's not from here," I pointed out.

"No. He's using us for his own glory, and we all know it. But being right doesn't always mean good, either."

Somewhere behind us, I swear to God, a few people struck up some music with the violins and a cello they'd brought.

"You know 'Nearer My God to Thee'?" I heard my father yell, and I could imagine my mother's elbow going into his ribs.

Miss Delacroix stepped closer to me, too close, and said, "I'll tell you this, Bud Castillo: if you are asked tonight to live forever, take the offer or you'll never see your friend again."

The party around us was a mixture between a potluck and a hoedown, at least how I imagined them. People danced and laughed, they played songs, they showed off the ears they could wiggle and the spoons they could hang off their noses. It would have been charming if it wasn't getting darker and colder with each passing minute.

I sat on the edges looking around for anything we could use to save them all. There had to be at least sixty, way too many for the three remaining wooden boats. Dad's Titanic joke seemed to be coming true.

When the darkness became complete and the stars shone faintly above us, the glowing arc lights of the rig made it seem a little like we were among them.

Pritchett didn't have to fire the gun this time to get attention. He stepped atop a crate and held his arms high.

"Can you feel that? The curtain of the universe is opening and it is time for us to take the stage!"

People gathered in a half circle to listen, my parents and I among them.

"We've been waiting in the wings a long time," Pritchett continued, always ready to squeeze a metaphor to death. "But now it is our cue to take our place in the spotlight. Our audience includes ancestors from the time when the sky was white all the way to the ones we loved in our own generation."

Folks applauded, some of them with tears in their eyes.

"We wouldn't be here without your faith in me, and I won't lie, your money as well. You hocked your unhappy lives in Galveston and Chicago and Omaha to come back here, and that was an act of bravery I will never forget. So thank you."

The applause came louder this time. Miss Delacroix shouted, "We'd give it again!" and Pritchett nodded.

"We also would be here without the Castillo family."

I'll confess, I was honored by the cheering that came next.

"Theodore Castillo, ladies and gentlemen, is a hero." Pritchett nodded. "He wouldn't say it aloud, but he is. The word 'hero' comes from the Greek for 'servant,' and though he didn't believe in our project, he believed in us and did it anyway."

A few hands came out of the crowd to slap Dad on the back and he smiled like a man in pain.

"And Virginia Castillo, the Jackie Kennedy of Innsmouth."

Mom narrowed her eyes as though trying to figure out if it was a compliment or not. Definitely a back-handed one.

"Class, distinction, intelligence, all in one package. And though she's feeling lost right now, we know she'll one day return to the art of bearing children."

It was my dad's turn to nudge her in the ribs when she took a step forward.

"And of course, young Theodore Junior, or as we call him,

Bud. He's a hero, too. He's done so much for our community. Step up here and take a bow."

I didn't want to, but hands from the crowd all but lifted me onto the crate with him.

"You all know this special young man." Pritchett's hands weighed on my shoulders. "But you don't REALLY know him. He's a boy of integrity. A true patriot. Trustworthy and loyal and...well, I'm sure he'll tell you all the rest."

People in the crowd were smiling at me. I tried to smile back, not sure if I succeeded.

"He thinks he wants to go back to New York, back to stickball and model airplanes and rescuing cats from trees. But he can't because that's not who he is anymore."

I suppose we all have a moment when we realize the door back to childhood has gotten narrower and shorter so we can no longer fit through. That was my moment, there on the rig. And I hated that Reverend Pritchett made me realize I'd lost it all forever.

You don't have to be good to be right.

"What he loves now is his friend Aubrey, the One Who Went First, blessed be the name. And what he doesn't know is I can grant him the wish he would never acknowledge, to camp and hike and live forever a Scout with his friend."

Did he mean heaven? Was he about to kill me?

"I wish I could tell you all what will happen next when we open the way. Some of us have enough of the blood to be welcomed home, and some don't. Some can be transformed, and some can't. I don't know the arts behind it, and I don't know the purposes of the Deep Ones. But I know it is worth the chance."

Many of the people were holding hands by then or clutching each other close. Mrs. Marsh stood with her arms folded, just like my dad.

Pritchett removed a black velvet cloth from the detonator stand, revealing the three switches. The crowd fell silent.

"Bud, as the purest among us, you are to be the Opener of the Way."

Up close, I could see the irony in his eyes. Fuck you, I thought.

"Oh, great Ones," he cried out toward the sea. "We come humbly to knock at thy gate. Will thee answer? Will thee take us to the shimmering home we've all seen in our dreams?"

I looked out at the remaining citizens of Innsmouth, the ones who had been too far away or too human to slip beneath the waves with their families, the ones who'd stalled and lived out among us on the land, fighting in a war like Colonel Marsh or writing for the papers like Miss Delacroix. They kept their photos and their keepsakes, and every night of their lives, they regretted that they weren't good enough to live forever.

They'd done what they could to live well instead, and they were still doing it, some with their fingers sticky from that night's lobster butter.

Maybe there was something under there, and maybe they could find their loved ones again. But I knew with an open door, the Deep Ones wouldn't stay here. They'd spread and find new places, and someday the world would be theirs.

A Scout is brave, I'd read once.

"No, thanks," I said.

Many of them gasped, but Mrs. Marsh yelled out, "Good boy!"

Pritchett nodded, and I knew what he would do next. I also knew I wouldn't be that night's reckless zealot for once.

He flipped the failsafe and then both explosive circuits at once.

18

Behind my closed eyes, I could almost see the signal shooting down the wire electron by electron, plunging down the copper under the waves and then to my father's carefully-placed charges and Primacord. I imagined it crackling across those tumbled rocks, passing them by to light the charges under the rig in a mushroom of bubbles.

I didn't have to imagine the plumes of sea water shooting toward the sky from three corners of the rig. The fourth came a few seconds later, maybe from a short. I wasn't caring much by then.

Thunder came from beneath our feet and the entire rig surged like it was trying to launch into the air. It seemed to slide and tilt, and then came this loud creaking like the world's largest squeaking screen door. Steel was ripping somewhere beneath us, and I had no idea where so we could run the other way.

People screamed and reached to one another for an impossible steadiness as the rig dropped out of plumb. The deck settled briefly at a 30 degree angle before descending to a 45 degree one, and everybody fell.

I looked for my mom and dad, and they'd both grabbed the railing where they'd positioned themselves. Dad caught sight of me and pointed at a set of cabinets about thirty feet away with the word CUIDADO on them.

I scrambled on all fours to get there, and when I did, I saw the latches were open from when my parents were sitting against them. I yanked one open and had an instant to see a stack of life jackets before something leaped for my face. I turned and it vaulted off my shoulder and splashed into the water.

Oh, I screamed. Believe me, I screamed. I also brushed off my shoulder frantically despite all the chaos around me.

"Rats!" I cried, as though it was the worst thing happening.

"Okay!" my father shouted, staggering out toward the people on the deck.

I began yanking out the jackets, all of them with stern warnings written on them in Spanish I couldn't read. Neither could my dad because his father never taught him any but the swears.

I flung them out behind me onto the grating, though about a third had been gnawed through as nests. Something flat and hairy and dead fell to my feet and I kicked it away.

"Ladies and gentlemen!" shouted Pritchett, holding his arms up with a deranged grin. "The time is—"

Dad shouldered into him and knocked him to the deck while Mom ran out waving her hands.

"Listen! Listen! Put on the life jackets and we'll carry you to shore!"

I began handing them out as best I could. By then, at least one of the pylons had collapsed and the rig was rotating to twist the others. There's no Engineering badge, but even I knew they'd snap before long.

Only half the people took the jackets I gave them. The others, some weeping, ran for the edge sinking toward the water. Mr. Olmstead paused, licked his lips, and then did a swan dive with twenty feet still between us and the sea.

"No!" I yelled, running toward them.

They pushed past me with desperation in their eyes, knocking me over.

Mrs. Marsh helped me to my feet and I felt her hands were half scaly, like someone who'd been burned.

"It is lies!" she yelled to the leapers. "They do not love!"

Either nobody heard or nobody cared. Miss Delacroix came next within arm's reach, and I managed to grab her arm.

"Don't," I said.

"He's down there," she shrieked. "He's been waiting."

"Miss Delacroix, he left you. He's an asshole."

She turned on me with a fierce look. "He can't be."

Her arm twisted from my grasp and she leaped off the side.

The thirty or so who wanted to live, at least for a few more years, were gathering at the highest corner with their life jackets on. A vibration pulsed from the deck and the rig turned more sharply. The lights flickered.

Farkas and Connaghan approached them, and the constable pulled his sad rusty little .38 from its holster.

I looked around for my dad and saw him struggling with Pritchett. I stepped closer to them but then stopped. Finally, I ran for Connaghan.

"Good people," Farkas was saying. "Don't let the fear of these people from Away deny you the life you were born to live."

Colliding with Connaghan was like diving into a ball of dough the size of a library globe. I doubt he even felt it.

He definitely felt the spear of rebar that Colonel Marsh used to puncture his side right beneath the arm. Connaghan pulled the trigger in a reflex, but the shot went high. I managed to grab the pistol and twist it out of his hand.

Farkas looked at me and then at the gun, which I wasn't even aiming at him. He backed away from me, clutching his briefcase, and then he dropped off the side to the ocean below without even a scream. I've wondered since how much legal work he planned to get down there if we'd broken through the reef.

I now stood on the deck of a sinking oil rig, a thirteen-year-old with a gun. Mom took it from my hand and to be honest, I was relieved. Castillo Syndrome and guns probably didn't mix.

Instead, I ran for where my father was still struggling with Pritchett.

The lights flickered, surged, and then went dark. The blackness around us was almost complete, with only the stars feebly trying to shine above us. I saw shadows wrestling before me, but I kept going.

I saw a flash from the muzzle of Pritchett's .357, followed by two more. Then a third and, a few seconds later, a fourth. One of the shadows fell to the deck, dragging the other atop him. There was no muzzle flash from the fifth shot, but a spray came out of the back of the man on top and then both were still. I wondered if that's what it had been like for the President a few weeks earlier.

Mom and I rushed up, and beneath the still flesh, we heard a muffled voice say, "Fuck!"

We peeled Pritchett's corpse off of my father.

"Fuck," he said again.

We helped my dad to his feet, but he stooped and panted to catch his breath.

"Get...a rope...and tie it into grips."

I didn't understand what he meant at first, but then I did. I found a line that was long enough, cut it with my knife, and then stood there with it stupidly.

Dad wanted people to be able to grab it and hold on, probably while we towed them to shore. I flipped in my mind through the types of knot I could use. A bowline? No, that was for the end.

I was lousy at knots, even in the light. I'd always hoped I wouldn't need them past earning the badge.

Pressure does weird things to your brain, though, and maybe some dollop of fat shook loose from a blood vessel somewhere so I could vaguely remember the butterfly knot.

"Start with an eight," Dad yelled, limping toward the ladder.

Yes, that was it. You twisted the line into a figure eight and then folded the top to the bottom. Then there was something and you had a butterfly knot. I tried through the upper loop but it fell apart. I started again and then put it through the lower opening instead.

I had a butterfly knot. Now I needed about twenty more.

So I stood in the dark, tying one after the other as evenly from both ends as I could, with just feel to guide me. Mr. Shattuck back in Queens, who thought I was hopeless, might even have been proud. I didn't give a shit at that moment.

"All right, sports fans," Dad shouted. "I need the ladyfolk to step down with me to the boats, and the menfolk to grab a loop in this rope. We're gonna pull you to shore."

"That water's gonna be colder than a witch's tit!" Mr. Pym said.

"Never felt one, but probably."

The rig dropped faster now, and the water was now about two inches deep above the deck. Three of the wooden boats were now clunking against the edge, straining on their moorings. I hurried over and cut the lines so they wouldn't be pulled down. Mom grabbed one line, Dad grabbed another, and I kept the third.

"Saddle up!"

The rope people came forward in a line and we hooked the middle of the rope to the transom so they'd be even behind us to steer straight.

The women stepped into the boat, though Mrs. Marsh waited.

"You too, ma'am," I said.

"I am a strong swimmer, like my boy," she said.

I wondered if he'd heard the explosion wherever he was down there, or if he was too far away either physically or mentally. If so, he might be the last survivor of Innsmouth, which was fine by me.

The water was now at our knees and someone said, "Oh, no."

Mrs. Marsh plunged into the water with an otherworldly grace. Colonel Marsh yelled after her, but she didn't surface again for about fifty feet.

When all the other women were aboard the three boats, Dad climbed into one and Mom took another. I got in the third.

None of those boats were seaworthy, but two of the motors started with a couple of pulls on the cord. Dad's took a few more but then it sputtered to life, too. Then came a cracking and a ripping and the transom splintered. The board spun as the motor dragged it to the bottom.

The stern tipped into the water.

"Jesus Christ," Dad said. "Everybody out!"

We managed to stuff all of the passengers in the other two boats which were now dangerously low to the water. The people huddled close to warm them.

Now we needed just two boat pilots.

"Okay, Bud, you get in," Mom said, stepping out of hers.

"No way."

"I was a lifeguard," she said, smiling.

"That lake was a quarter mile wide," Dad said. I learned later that he knew because he'd been there in the Catskills, working as a waiter. It was where they'd met.

"I have the Mile Swim badge," I pointed out.

"Bud, you know my book you took?"

She knew I had her copy of *The Feminine Mystique*? That was embarrassing.

"I can do things, too," she said.

I glanced back at the people sinking now, some already treading water. All I'd learned about being a boy and a man said women should be taken care of, but I guess I was learning some handbooks are truer than others.

I climbed into her boat and took the steering handle. Mom inched into the water and then lowered herself like someone settling into a bath.

"Bracing," she said, and a few of the men laughed.

We looped the middle of the rope onto my boat and tipped our motors so the propellers churned the water. We surged forward, and behind us the Maracaibo Explorer gave one final groan as though glad to be rid of us. From the toppling control room, I could hear the ringing of a phone, but I knew it wasn't for any of us. The ringing stopped when the rig slipped beneath the surface, leaving behind only the tall crane with the drill.

It was resting, all hundred tons of it, on top of Devil's Reef—sealing it for a long time to come.

Small favors, I thought.

"All right," Dad shouted. "Lead the way."

The sea was black with a few stars blinking behind the incoming clouds.

"Which way?"

"West," he yelled.

Behind me, the rig had twisted so much from its moorings that I couldn't rely on it as a navigation reference.

"Use the stars," Dad yelled again.

"I don't know how!" I could never see them like that in Queens.

We went forward another minute, with no idea if forward was north or south or maybe even out further to sea.

To my left, though, one star flashed at the corner of my vision. It kept flashing in a way that stars normally don't and at an altitude that stars normally aren't, and I realized it was someone holding up a military surplus flashlight with all the extra lenses.

There was a Scout in the water to lead us home.

We steered toward him, and a few people grunted behind me as the rope pulled taut. I was careful not to go too fast, and I checked back often to see if anyone had fallen away. Mom had taken the last loop, though, to make sure no one did.

Cold shock, I thought. Heart attack, I thought.

I focused ahead toward the tiny light, and the noise of the

breakers assured me we were navigating true.

On Dad's boat, I saw him leaning to one side, and someone pulled him straight again and then down. I thought again of President Kennedy, lying on the floor of the limousine in Dallas, and I wanted to crank the throttle to get to him faster, but I couldn't.

We reached the shore in twenty minutes, and the men on the rope climbed up the ladders of the docks. Someone helped my mother up rather chivalrously, but she let him. Still in the water, though, Mr. Pym hung loosely to his rope handle. He'd died somewhere along the way.

While they pulled him out, I leaped from the boat and splashed in the shallows toward my Dad's. Aubrey followed in big loping steps as though he didn't quite have feet anymore, which I guessed he didn't. I could have hugged him or even kissed him, but Mrs. Marsh had emerged and was already trying to do that.

Aubrey, still at least partly a boy, hunched but let her. I noticed he wore my mother's kerchief around his scaled neck, just below the gills.

Dad was in the bottom of the boat all right, and the women were climbing out of the way when we got in. They gasped to see Aubrey, but not with too much surprise.

"Goddamn," Dad muttered. "Killed by an American." He coughed. "Sort of."

"You haven't been killed," I said, opening his coat and then his shirt to feel for where he'd been shot. I found two punctures sticky with blood.

Aubrey elevated his feet in the classic position to treat shock, and someone rushed over with a coarse woolen blanket. Mom ran to our side and knelt beside him, still soaked to the bone with blue lips.

Heart attack, I thought, ready to pull her away.

"The wounds might not be mortal," Aubrey said. His voice was deeper but garbled by some viscous fluid now always in his throat.

"Oh, they feel mortal," Dad said.

Dr. Brunner staggered along the dock, probably in shock of his own. Every dream he'd had for a new species of man was now pinned by steel and rubble in Innsmouth Harbor. His eyes showed it, too, the death of a dreamer.

Mom looked up, shivering now. With a shaking hand, she aimed Connaghan's revolver at him, barely holding it steady.

Brunner froze.

"Save him or you're dead," she said as loud as she could.

He might not have heard her, but he felt the survivors of Innsmouth closing in around him to do worse than any bullet.

He hurried over and knelt beside my father.

"I don't know if—"

Mom pulled back the hammer, though it took her other hand to do it.

"Let's see what we can do," he said, reaching beneath the blanket.

19

Some of the townsfolk hurried to their darkened houses and came back with blankets for Mom and the other swimmers, and as a crowd, they limped toward Dr. Brunner's office with my dad on a makeshift stretcher. I wanted badly to follow, but one more person wouldn't help. It didn't even occur to me that I'd have to say goodbye to my father because I knew another one had to come first.

Aubrey slid back into the water with his head showing above the surface, and I stooped beside him at the dock.

I wasn't sure what to say or what to do. My best friend, then or ever, was about to go places I never could, and I'd go places he never could. In just over half a decade, I'd be in Vietnam, looking for him in the waters of the Gulf of Tonkin. Not long after, I'd be in San Francisco and looking for him in the bay by the Golden Gate.

And someday I'd be in Florida after medical school with my family, walking the beaches of Clearwater where it was never cold and gray like Innsmouth. And I'd look for him there, because he'd taught me all I needed to know about saving the good people instead of always fighting the bad ones.

I knew none of that then, and my throat was too tight to say it if I had.

He seemed to understand.

"Your dad has a good chance," he said. "Most of those wounds were in the side, and he was pretty bundled up."

"Yeah." I wasn't as sure, but it was out of my hands.

"I'm glad you came here."

I nodded. "Me, too."

"I got to be a Scout."

"You still are."

"And a boy."

"You might not still be that," I said, and he grinned with his wide mouth.

"I'm not sure you are, either."

I rubbed my dripping nose with the sleeve of my shirt.

"What are you going to do?"

He considered a moment and then tilted his head. "I think I'm going on the longest campout ever."

I hoped so with all my heart.

"Can I keep…" he tugged at the kerchief my mother had given him.

"It's yours," I said.

"Good. I want to remember." He looked back toward the sea like someone regretful that his ride had come and the night was over.

"Maybe I'll see you," I said.

"Stay close to the shore and you might."

We didn't speak for a moment.

"I have to…"

I nodded.

He held up his hand, bent awkwardly as best he could with the webbed fingers into a Scout salute. I returned it with one of my own.

"Goodbye," I said, but by then, he was plunging under the water like someone who'd lived there all his life.

20

The Scout Handbook can tell you how to roll your socks for a campout, but it's got nothing about how to blow up an oil rig, thwart a madman intent on reuniting with an ancient degenerate tribe of sea beings, or rescue your mom from matronly New Englanders. There's no checklist to pack for a water rescue, no procedure for saving someone from gunshot wounds, and definitely no advice for beginning again with nothing.

We had to figure out all that useful stuff on our own.

My dad survived Innsmouth, believe it or not, though not for long. He passed in 1970 when I started college after a tour in my generation's war. We didn't win ours like his did, but I'm not sure that changed the way we felt about doing it. Dad didn't want me to go because he knew even winning wasn't always winning.

My mom made it all the way to 2016, and of course it was the cigarettes that got her when the cancer metastasized from her lungs into a perfect little golf ball in her brain. You wouldn't think it could happen with a physician for a son, but it can. She said the coffin nails helped her work, and that work at an ad agency kept her living in a nice duplex in Queens until she retired to move near us in Florida, as all the handbooks say people her age must do.

I've still got Mom's copy of the Friedan book somewhere.

In the end, we saved thirty-eight out of sixty people from Innsmouth, a number I've always been ashamed of. Yes, a lot of them went to the bottom willingly where they were surprised by the sealed reef awaiting them, but too many were simply unable to bear the stress or the cold or the broken hearts.

Where the survivors went, I wish I knew. I hope Dr. Brunner didn't find a new audience for his bullshit, but guys like him have a way of finding their kind. We got Christmas cards from the Spivey sisters up until the mid-Seventies, so I'm guessing that's when one or both of them passed. I'm sure the others ended up in nursing homes and hospices with some strange stories to tell and maybe an affinity for Fish Fridays in the cafeteria.

I never went past First Class Scout, never got Star, never earned Life, and never achieved Eagle. Not because the book was full of shit but because too many people were. There are handbooks and handbooks, right? Some on the inside and some on the out.

What's funny is these days in my retirement, I'm wading out a little further each day into the surf during my walks on the beach. There's nice warm sand out there on Sanibel, much kinder on the feet than the rocks of Innsmouth ever were. I let my hands trail along the shimmering surface while the water rises past my belly to my chest, and even one day last week to my neck while I swirled my arms to stay afloat.

I don't think I'm seriously considering diving underneath

forever yet. My family would miss me, and I'm still enjoying the sun. But if I ever see someone peer out from below with wide glimmering eyes and a kerchief around his neck, I make no promises.

Author's Note

When I was nine years old, my father gave me a copy of the 1963 *Boy Scout Handbook* with the same Norman Rockwell cover that Bud describes in the second paragraph of this story. That copy wasn't my father's, though he and my grandfather had both been Scouts; it's more likely that someone brought it to trade at the bookstore my parents briefly owned, and my father thought it might make me a bit less strange.

As you can tell from the book you're holding in your hands, that plan backfired spectacularly.

By the time he gave it to me, I was already the kind of kid who took books way more seriously than most people. To me, every book was a handbook, teaching you something about how to live by positive or negative example, and the line between fiction and non-fiction was blurry for me. Living with my father's mercurial and violent moods had trained me to be an agile reconciler of opposing ideas.

You know, like placing a Boy Scout in Lovecraft's Innsmouth.

I believed in the books I read about vampires and UFOs and gnomes living in the woods, and I wondered why nobody else did. When I was finally old enough to join the real Boy Scouts, I didn't understand why all the other Scouts wanted to run around in camouflage in the woods and burn things instead of living up to the ideals of being trustworthy, loyal, helpful, friendly, courteous, kind, obedient, cheerful, thrifty, brave, clean, and reverent.

Which I just typed from memory forty years later.

Even today, I'm puzzled by how we have thousands of years of books that tell us how to live as decent people, but we just decide not to do it. Our ancestors suffered enormously to learn those lessons, but we don't believe them until we burn ourselves on the stove.

I was more or less destined to one day write a book about how if books are bullshit, that's more our fault than theirs. It's my message back in time to that kid in the 80s who lived mentally in the 60s and didn't understand why nobody built soap box derby cars or model railroads anymore. Or why he couldn't stop his father from being so destructive or his mother so scared.

It's natural to ask how a person who all but lived inside that Scout handbook never made it to Eagle Scout, and the answer is a fistfight.

As my parents' marriage was (thankfully) falling apart and we moved farther away from my Scout troop, I had to step down from my position as Senior Patrol Leader (the kid who led meetings and activities). The truth was that I was too young to be in that position, much younger than many of the other kids, and it was just as well for all of us that I didn't have to persuade people to do the right thing anymore.

One meeting soon after my tenure, the new Senior Patrol Leader and his buddies were horsing around in the Scout Hut, tackling each other, and I asked somewhat pointedly if we were going to actually have a meeting.

One of the Senior Patrol Leader's minions walked up to me, shoved my shoulder, and asked why I even cared. It wasn't like I was in charge anymore.

That kid's timing wasn't good. I was being bullied at my new school, not to mention for the last twelve years by my father, and I'd refused to ever fight back (partly thanks to the principles of the Scout Handbook). I used to run home from the bus stop after school, and I'd never swung my fist at any of the kids who were chasing me.

For some reason, a Scout meeting with my father sitting in the back room with the other adult leaders seemed like a perfect time to change that.

I wish I could say that I raised my fists like Rocky and laid that kid out with a right hook, but really it was more of a long arcing slap that got him in the side of the head, smashing his glasses.

In the ensuing fracas, one kid grabbed my arms from behind to stop the fight (or, more accurately, me from fighting), but I got an arm free and smacked him somehow, too. The adults began to emerge, including my father. He walked up to me, put his hand on my shoulder, and turned to the Scoutmaster.

"My son and I resign," he said, steering me out of the building.

The kid with the broken glasses walked up to him and opened his mouth to ask about getting them replaced, but the look my father gave him over his own reading glasses made him shrink back.

I cried the whole way home, assuming that I'd destroyed my Boy Scout career and my father would be furious. Instead, he stopped at a gas station, bought me a Three Musketeers, and said, "You did good."

My father was gone from our lives with a new wife and new crimes less than a year later, but I remember that as one moment when his antisocial personality disorder was a little useful and inspiring for a change.

I went back to a new Scout troop a few times after that, but it never felt right. I stalled out at the Life rank just below Eagle for several reasons, including my fear of leading other boys in a final community service project.

I guess this book is that project. I hope you enjoy it, and I hope it's a handbook of sorts for you, though maybe it's one you shouldn't take too seriously.

Until you have to.

Will Ludwigsen
Willow Branch Library
November 2023

Acknowledgments

I first thought of the idea for this book—"Boy Scouts...in Innsmouth!"—in September of 2001. Like a shoggoth, it has taken many different terrifying forms between then and now, and many people have helped it evolve through each one.

President, CEO, and founder of Lethe Press Steve Berman has always been a believer in this story even when I wasn't, and this book is in your hands largely because of him. He encouraged me to keep going and pulled out all the stops for publishing it, including asking Jeremy John Parker to bring it to life with his brilliant cover and design. I'm grateful for them both.

My father gave me a 1963 edition of the *Boy Scout Handbook*, hoping to make me a real man who enjoyed the outdoors. Instead, he created a stunned idealist who still doesn't understand the gap between books and reality. So, uh, thanks for that, I guess?

My original Scouting experience came from Troop 26 in Englewood, Florida with Eric Jeske, John Antes, Morgan Jones, Ricky and Robbie Schultz, Bryon Raker, Dan Hoven, Mark and Eric Botelho, and Rick Raver. If any of them remember me at all, it's probably as a shrill martinet of the Scout handbook, but I was glad for their company. Thanks, also, to our adult leaders, including our improbably named Scoutmaster Dick Raver.

Much of this book was written at the Stonecoast MFA program at the University of Southern Maine, and many excellent writers provided valuable feedback for that stage of its development. I'm especially grateful to Angela Still, Robert Stutts, Nellie Dilger, Kevin St. Jarre, Jenn Brissett, Paul Kirsch, and Zack Jernigan for their insights. Also my mentors Mike Kimball, Elizabeth Hand, and Jim "Does It Have to Be in Innsmouth?" Kelly made a huge difference to the story and my own development as a writer. Jim, your question sparked a very necessary circuitous path, much like a hike in the woods. I appreciate it.

Many friends have heard fragments of this story over the years around our Willcon campfires, and I appreciate the patient indulgence of Scott McClellan, Don Rochester, Tom Phillips, Ray Rodil, Ray Champion, Jason Carroway, Thad Smith, John Lewis, Mark Boehnke, Kelley Vanda, Arnold Cassell, Mac Mc-Donald, Nell and Debbie Phillips, and Chris Harben.

I also award a Special Merit Badge of Honor/Horror to Tony Tucker who played a *Call of Cthulhu* adventure I ran based on this story and called it "the most disturbing thing I've ever played."

Aubrey Marsh has a lot of complicated DNA, not just from his Lovecraftian heritage but also from two friends over the years who modeled his creed of curiosity, courage, and bohemian independence: Norman Amemiya and William Simmons. You both were/are fellow Scouts in arms.

Thanks, also, to the colleagues at my day job who made it safe to be odd and relieved me of having to choose between my art and my career. Dana Syme, Heidi Burgess, Marjorie Newell, Nicelle Ambo, Chip Tran, Pamela Boggs, and of course my boss Pete Martinez showed me that creativity at the office feeds creativity at home. Thanks to Amy Schneider and Amy Herron, I may have more readers among senior corporate leaders than I do in the horror community. Which is great, because those leaders have more money.

Of course my family's support made it possible both to become a Scout and then to realize that I could hike my own path. My mother, Dianne Hall, and stepfather Larry Hall inspired me to be a Scout of the weird, and I hope they'd like this version of a story they read long ago before they passed away. My sister, Karen Simpson, and brother-in-law Marty Simpson have always encouraged my writing. My nieces Katie and Emily show me what real talent is every day, forcing me to keep up. My brother Andrew Hall has inspired me with his pride that I create peculiar shit like this.

Aimee Payne has endured (perhaps even enjoyed?) nearly twenty years of me both writing and living weird fiction. It's no coincidence that the quality and quantity of my work soared after her advent in my life, so you have her to thank if you've enjoyed it. I certainly have.

About the Author

Will Ludwigsen's stories of strange mystery have appeared in eclectic venues like *Asimov's Science Fiction*, *Alfred Hitchcock's Mystery Magazine*, *Weird Tales*, *Nightmare Magazine*, *Cemetery Dance*, and *The Year's Best Science Fiction and Fantasy*, among many other places. His collection, *In Search Of and Others*, was a finalist for the Shirley Jackson Award.

Will earned his Master of Fine Arts in Creative Writing from the University of Southern Maine and taught genre creative writing at the University of North Florida. When he isn't reconciling the eerie with the absurd as a corporate education writer, he's doing it for you in his fiction.

Will lives and writes in Jacksonville, FL, with his partner Aimee Payne, also a writer.

Yes, he was a Boy Scout who took it way too seriously.

You can follow him online at www.will-ludwigsen.com.

About the Type

This book is typeset in IM Fell Double Pica, a modern revival font based on The Fell Types which take their name from John Fell, a Bishop of Oxford in the seventeenth-century. The original typecase was cut by Peter de Walpergen in 1684 then digitally reproduced by Igino Marini, an Italian civil engineer, starting in the year 2000.

The cover fonts are **JOHN MUIR SANS**, a versatile, rough, and worn sans serif font inspired by vintage National Parks poster fonts, the National Forest Service, and the iconic John Muir himself, designed by Vicarel Studios and **National Forest Regular**, a font inspired by the National Park Service signs made using a router bit to put the timeless nostalgia of national park signs into a digital typeface, designed by Rachel Kick.